PITS AND PIECES OF MURDER

A BARKSIDE OF THE MOON COZY MYSTERY
BOOK 7

RENEE GEORGE

BARKSIDE OF THE MOON PRESS

Pits and Pieces of Murder

A Barkside of the Moon Cozy Mystery Book 7

Copyright © 2022 by Renee George

All rights reserved. No part of this publication may be reproduced, stored in a retrieval system, or transmitted, in any form or by any means, without the prior permission in writing of the copyright holder.

Any trademarks, service marks, product names or named features are assumed to be the property of their respective owners, and are used only for reference. There is no implied endorsement by the author of this work.

This is a work of fiction. All characters and storylines in this book are inspired only by the author's imagination. The characters are based solely in fiction and are in no relation inspired by anyone bearing the same name or names. Any similarities to real persons, situations, or incidents is purely coincidental.

Print ISBN: 978-1-947177-42-0

Publisher: Barkside of the Moon Press

PARANORMAL MYSTERIES & ROMANCES
BY RENEE GEORGE

Grimoires of a Middle-aged Witch
https://www.renee-george.com/GMW
Earth Spells Are Easy
Spell On Fire
When the Spells Blows
Spell Over Troubled Water
Ghost in the Spell

Nora Black Midlife Psychic Mysteries
www.norablackmysteries.com
Sense & Scent Ability (Book 1)
For Whom the Smell Tolls (Book 2)
War of the Noses (Book 3)
Aroma With A View (Book 4)
Spice and Prejudice (Book 5)
The Age of Inno-Scents (Book 6)

Peculiar Mysteries
www.peculiarmysteries.com

You've Got Tail (Book 1)
My Furry Valentine (Book 2)
Thank You For Not Shifting (Book 3)
My Hairy Halloween (Book 4)
In the Midnight Howl (Book 5)
My Peculiar Road Trip (Magic & Mayhem) (Book 6)
Furred Lines (Book 7)
My Wolfy Wedding (Book 8)
Who Let The Wolves Out? (Book 9)
My Thanksgiving Faux Paw (Book 10)

Witchin' Impossible Cozy Mysteries

www.witchinimpossible.com
Witchin' Impossible (Book 1)
Rogue Coven (Book 2)
Familiar Protocol (Booke 3)
Mr & Mrs. Shift (Book 4)

Barkside of the Moon Mysteries

www.barksideofthemoonmysteries.com
Pit Perfect Murder (Book 1)
Murder & The Money Pit (Book 2)
The Pit List Murders (Book 3)
Pit & Miss Murder (Book 4)
The Prune Pit Murder (Book 5)
Two Pits and A Little Murder (Book 6)
Pits and Pieces of Murder (Book 7)

Madder Than Hell

www.madder-than-hell.com
Gone With The Minion (Book 1)

Devil On A Hot Tin Roof (Book 2)
A Street Car Named Demonic (Book 3)

Hex Drive
https://www.renee-george.com/hex-drive-series
Hex Me, Baby, One More Time (Book 1)
Oops, I Hexed It Again (Book 2)
I Want Your Hex (Book 3)
Hex Me With Your Best Shot (Book 4)

ACKNOWLEDGMENTS

I have to thank my BFFs Sister Robbin and Robyn Peterman for helping me get to THE END! You two are the bread to my jam. And thank you to my husband for putting up with my grumpiness and lack of sleep as I barreled toward my deadline. He'll be happy to know that hygiene is back on he menu. LOL.

To the fans of Lily and Smooshie, as you know, these stories are love letter"s to my obsession with whodunits and my obsession with my pit bull Kona. Thank you for taking this ride with me! <3

Last, I want to thank that hot, super charged, sexy as sin coffee for firing up the muse. Thank you, Coffee. I couldn't do this without you.

Also, if you are interested in rescue dogs, I encourage you to look into your local shelters.

If you don't have a favorite, here's mine: (www.mopitbullrescue.org) If you can, please donate as they expand their new shelter that will allow them to house even more rescues until they can be placed in foster or forever homes.

For Kona, Simon, and Ash.

BLURB

A blizzard, a body (or two), and another mystery to solve.

When Lily Mason and her friends go on a winter holiday to a pet-friendly mountain resort, no one expects murder to be on the weekend's agenda. Things get twisted, when Lily and company discover the victim is no victim, and the suspects all have a reason for wanting him dead.

When a blizzard strands them all on the mountain, and a guest goes missing, the Moonrise gang kicks their investigation into high gear. They will have to pull out all the tricks if they are to have a snowball's chance of solving the murder, before the killer can claim another victim.

CHAPTER 1

Crisp white snow blanketed the ground at Waggin' Trails, a pet-friendly resort near the top of Slowpark Mountain in northern Missouri. Parker Knowles, my hot husband, and I, along with our extended family, had booked a cabin for a glorious work-free four-day weekend at the end of February. We'd arrived at noon, threw our suitcases inside our cozy cabin, and rushed outside for some good old-fashioned winter fun. The blazing sun made the snowy landscape blindingly bright, which was the only excuse I had for nailing Parker Knowles, the great love of my life, right in the face with an icy snowball.

He spun as the deadly ball smacked him in the cheek, and he hit the ground with a grunt.

"Oh, no!" I raced the short fifteen feet to him. "Parker." He didn't move. I dropped to my knees and rolled him over. "Parker!" I was so scared that I'd hurt him I didn't notice his right hand moving until he smashed a handful of packed snow right down the front of my jacket.

"Gotcha, Lily!"

I laughed at the end of a scream as I scrambled away, unzipping my coat as the freezing slush slid down to my belly button.

Parker, with a bright red mark on his face, laughed and laughed as I danced around.

I retrieved a clump of snow that had broken off from the ball and had gotten trapped in my bra. "You are totally going down."

"I'm pretty sure that's what just happened." He touched his swelling cheek.

"I'm sorry." I jutted my lower lip into a pout as I shook the rest of the snow out of my shirt. "I didn't mean to hit you that hard."

He got up and grabbed either side of my open coat, and tugged me to him. Where my skin had been chilly moments earlier, it was heating up now. Parker kissed me, his blue eyes sparkling with mischief. "If I had known putting snow down your top would get you out of your clothes...."

I giggled. "All you have to do is ask."

We were perched on a slight incline, so when Smooshie, my seventy-five-pound red and white pit bull, sprinted across the yard and planted her feet on my butt, Parker and I fell head over heels—not metaphorically—down the slippery slope. I was spitting ice by the time a courteous evergreen stopped our descent. Elvis, Parker's one-hundred-and-fifty-pound pit bull-Great Dane mix, barked a warning alert.

"Too late," Parker said loudly to his good boy. "Many seconds too late."

Smooshie had followed us down the hill and proceeded to lick the snow off my brows. I peered at Parker out of one squinted eye since the other had a dog tongue covering it. "I don't think we're getting naked anytime soon."

"That's all right," he said, reaching over me and giving Smooshie an ear scritch. "We have a whole four days of vacation. Naked time is going to happen."

I kissed him. "I like your optimism."

He reached down and zipped up my coat. "You have to be freezing."

"Not too bad," I said. "Shifters run hot."

"Ain't that the truth," he countered.

Euphemism aside, it was the truth. I'm a werecougar—a shapeshifter who can change into a cougar. As such, I'm stronger than the average human, I live longer, and my body temperature runs high. Thanks to the original magic that had created my species, I'm also resilient.

"Hey, you two." My bestie Nadine Booth was at the top of the hill, pushing an inline stroller-for-three designed for all-terrain. Buzz Mason, my uncle and only living relative, stood next to her. Nadine had given birth to their three bundles of joy—two boys, Jackson and Jericho, and a girl, Journey—the previous March. Their babies had arrived a few weeks early and via C-section, but all of them, including Mom, had come out of the procedure happy and healthy. "We're taking the triplets on a walk to do some exploring. Do you guys want to come along?"

"Absolutely," I said, bouncing up. I grabbed Parker's hand and dragged him up to his feet. I dusted the snow from my pants. "We're in."

"Just give me a minute to get the dogs' leashes," I told her.

Smooshie excitedly yipped as she raced with us up the hill.

The rustically decorated cabin featured exposed wall beams, natural wood fixtures, and cozy furniture dressed with hand-stitched quilts. It had one bedroom downstairs and two up, all with their own private bathrooms. The ground floor bedroom was the largest, so we all agreed that Buzz, Nadine, and the babies should have that room. The kitchen and dining room were separated from the living room with a staircase that split the shared spaces in half.

The Ferrars, aka Greer and Reggie's pit bulls Elinor and Edward, curled up in front of the living room fireplace. Reggie and Greer were snuggled on the couch. Greer, who was Parker's dad, glanced over his shoulder at me.

"You guys want to go on an adventure?" I asked.

"It was a long ride," Reggie lamented. Reggie Crawford was a doctor in Moonrise, and when there was a suspicious death, she also acted as the medical examiner for the county. She pushed back her long, straight black hair and smiled wanly at me. "We're going to hang out here and enjoy the fire."

"Sounds good," I told them. "You want us to take the dogs?"

Greer smirked. "I think they're happy where they are."

I grabbed Smooshie and Elvis's leashes from the coat hooks mounted near the door. "You two enjoy."

Smooshie and Elvis were in their winter vests on the covered porch, sitting next to a standing Parker. Elvis was calm, but Smoosh, her thick tail whacking the porch floor and her body shaking with barely contained joy, looked anything but Zen.

Parker had his hands on both their heads. His dark hair and bright blue eyes never failed to make me swoon. He wasn't an extremely tall man, only five-eleven, but I was short at only five-one, so I had to raise up on my tiptoes to greet him with a kiss. Even then, he had to dip his head to meet me halfway.

"You ready?" he asked. He brought my hand to his lips and pressed a kiss to the ring on my left ring finger. It was a simple gold band inscribed with our names and one of the vows from our handfasting, *Parker and Lily...through sunshine and rain*. It was Parker's post-wedding gift to me, and I never took it off unless I was shifting, and then, I kept it on a chain that I could wear around my neck.

I loved the reminder that Parker was mine and I was his.

"Come on, you two," Buzz shouted from the road. "We're burning daylight."

"Coming," I hollered to Buzz and Nadine.

I handed Parker Elvis's leash, then clipped Smooshie's onto her thick collar. I wrapped the cord around her waist then pulled it through the loop near the collar clip. The heavy-duty leash acted as a harness that would give her chest a squeeze if she needed managing on the walk. We used them at the rescue for their toughness and because they were humane.

The gravel road leading to the cabin had been salted, so the tire grooves were slushy. We stayed to the outside of the tracks. The crisp air added to my own excitement. Smooshie trotted to the side of the road and walk-squatted, leaving a ragged yellow trail in the snow.

Parker nudged me with his shoulder. "What's got you smiling?"

"All this snow reminds me of my first winter in Moonrise."

He raised a brow. "Which part? The dead body or me being arrested?"

I rolled my eyes. "The part where Smooshie pushed me out of the way of an oncoming car, and you helped me to my feet. You both saved my life that day."

"Smooshie did all the work," he said fondly.

"Yeah, but you fed me and gave me a warm place to stay, even though you didn't know me."

He slipped his hand into mine. "I knew you the moment I saw you," he said. "And for the record, you saved my life, too, Lily."

I knew what he meant. Before I'd arrived, Parker's PTSD from his time in the military had been unpredictable. Elvis, his service dog, had helped him manage day-to-day, but since we'd been together, Parker had needed Elvis less and less. At least for his PTSD.

During my four years at the pit bull rescue, I discovered that there was something in my DNA as a shifter that had a calming effect on dogs. My mojo made rescuing scared dogs less scary for both parties. I went out on almost every call now, especially if abuse was involved. Parker claims my mojo works on humans, too. But I'd been attacked and shot at enough to know that wasn't true. However, my calming presence did seem to work on him. But Parker was my mate. His mind, his soul, his body, and his scent were tied to me, not just on an emotional level but also on a cellular one. Still, it didn't mean he didn't need Elvis. Like Smooshie, the big, loveable lug would always be important, just not for the same reasons.

Since Buzz, who was also a werecougar, didn't put off the same calming vibe, I often wondered if it had anything to do with my great-grandmother, on my mother's side, being a witch. Her magic had been better than any truth serum, and I'd inherited a little of that from her. People found it near impossible to lie when I asked them a direct question. I couldn't tell you how often friends and strangers poured out their long-held secrets to me without much prompting, like the time Opal Dixon told me about shooting her younger sister Pearl's mob-connected abusive husband and absconding with his money.

Anyhow, I'd learned over the past couple of years since the gift manifested that I had to be careful about how and why I asked personal questions.

"I'm so glad we decided to do this," I said. "We should check out the skiing when we get to the lodge."

"Sounds good to me," Nadine said. "Are you sure Greer's not going to mind watching the kids?"

"Dad broke his leg in a skiing accident. He's got no use for it now," Parker told her.

"Yeah, but he said that was twenty years ago. He might feel differently now," she pointed out.

Even if Greer had wanted to go skiing, I knew he'd pick watching the triplets over the activity. Those three babies were the closest he would ever get to grandchildren. He'd been accepting of the fact that Parker and I didn't want any babies of our own. Our dogs and the other rescues were all the kids and extra responsibility we needed. Even so, I think he had always thought he'd have grandkids one day. Buzz and Nadine had filled that hole for him.

"He's going to spoil them rotten while we're on the slopes," I said.

"Slope," Buzz corrected me. "Singular."

"There might only be one big slope, but there are a couple of bunny slopes, and those are the ones I plan to play on until I get the hang of balancing on two sticks." I stuck my tongue out at him. "Some of us don't have any experience with extracurricular activities."

I'd only been seventeen when my parents died, and I'd raised my brother from the time he was seven years old until he was out of school. The responsibility of Danny had fallen square on my shoulders. Which meant there was never enough money or time to do things like ski vacations.

Parker looped his arm around my shoulders. "I'm happy to hang out on the bunny slopes with you, darling." He kissed my temple. "But I have a feeling you'll be flying down the big hill after a lesson or two. You'll be flying circles around us."

"Only if I manage to sprout wings." I laughed. "Unfortunately, I'm furred and not feathered."

Buzz gave a low grunt when a man and a woman rounded the bend ahead of us. We were shapeshifters living in a human world, and he always worried about the ramifications if we were found out by the wrong people. Now that he and Nadine had children, I knew his fear had tripled.

The fortyish man had dark brown hair with a close-cropped salt and pepper beard. He wore a black parka, gray ski pants, and black boots. The woman, who looked younger, had her light brown hair down past her shoulders, and she wore cream from head to toe, including her knitted cap. They were arguing in low voices, but one of the benefits of being a werecougar was extremely good hearing.

"Why did we have to leave? We had the whole slope to ourselves for another hour," the woman protested. "I can't help if someone is nice to me."

"You were practically throwing yourself at him," the man snapped. "And he was all over you."

"That's his job," she protested. "He only grabbed me to keep me from busting my butt."

The man started to say something more, but then he saw us. He put his arm around the woman possessively and pasted on a smile that managed to look almost genuine.

"Howdy, folks," he said genially as we got closer. "Nice day for it."

"Sure is," Buzz said, just as friendly.

The woman with him wasn't quite as good at faking it. Her smile didn't reach her eyes. She peeked over at the babies when they were crossing our path. "Beautiful sweethearts."

Smooshie, who had developed quite the mamma complex around the triplets, inserted herself between the woman and the stroller. Smooshie wasn't being aggressive so much as she just wanted strangers to know that the three tykes were hers.

The woman's large tote bag began to growl and bark in high yips. She unzipped the top, and a small, fuzzy black and white dog popped its head up. Its whole body vibrated with alarm.

"It's alright, Milo." She petted his small head. "Mommy's making new friends."

"Mommy's good at that," the man grumbled. When he caught my gaze, he smiled again.

I ignored him. "Cute pup," I said. "What kind is he?"

"He's a Bichon Frise," she said proudly. "Your dogs are cute too."

Smooshie, as if knowing she was being complimented, turned in a circle to show off her wiggle butt.

The woman laughed then asked, "Are you all heading up to the lodge?"

"Yep," I said. "We just got here this morning, so we're still checking the place out."

"The restaurant serves a really good Cuban sandwich," she said. "I'm Cat Maddox, by the way." She shook her head with a chuckle. "I'm a Cat who loves dogs, ironic, huh?"

Since I literally shifted into a giant cat and I loved dogs, too, I didn't think it was all that ironic. Still, I grinned at her joke.

She pointed at the man. "This is my husband, Dade. We've been here since last Friday."

"I'm Lily." I gestured with my head as I made introductions all around. "That's Parker, Buzz, Nadine, and these three wonders are Jack, Jericho, and Journey."

"They are the sweetest," Cat said. "I can't wait to have my own one day. Maybe not three at once, though."

Nadine chuckled. "I can't say I recommend it, but these guys are totally worth it."

"Well, it was nice talking to you folks, but we should be going." Dade tugged on his wife's arm.

She gave him a hard look then said to Nadine and me. "We're in cabin seven, and we'll be here for another week. You two should come down for a glass of wine sometime."

"Thanks," I said. "Maybe we'll do that." Though I had no intention of following through. We only had four days, and I planned to spend all my time with the people I loved.

After Cat and Dade passed us, I heard Dade hiss at his wife, "Embarrass me like that again, and I'll make you sorry."

I didn't detect any lie, and I worried for the woman, even if I didn't know her. I stopped short and turned on my heel. "Cat," I yelled. "How about I stop by tomorrow around one?"

Parker furrowed his brow as he focused on me with a confused gaze. I gave the barest shake of my head, and he shrugged. I wanted Dade to know that someone would be checking in on his wife.

Cat smiled. "It's a date."

CHAPTER 2

The lodge wasn't what you'd call fancy, but it had charm. Like our accommodations, it had a log cabin design. Only, the lodge boasted forty hotel rooms, a fine dining restaurant, a bar and grill, a spa, a fitness room, and an indoor pool complete with a hot tub and sauna. There was a doggy daycare for people who couldn't leave their pets in their rooms or cabins when they wanted to visit or use any of the community areas, including the slopes.

Billy Brandish, the resort's manager, waved at us from the front steps. When he'd checked us in earlier, he'd insisted we call him Billy.

"Howdy, folks." Billy was tall with light brown hair. He looked to be in his forties, and he was impeccably groomed—clean shaven, no hair out of place, and manicured nails. However, there was something about him that was a little...oily for my taste. "Did you get settled into your cabin okay?"

"It's perfect," I told him. Smooshie yanked me

forward as she sniffed around Billy's legs. I pulled her back. "Sorry about that."

He laughed. "No worries. She is probably smelling my girl Tilly on my pants." He nodded to Smooshie. "She's a beauty." He glanced at Elvis. "And that's one handsome guy."

Parker's shoulders straightened, and the hint of a smile on his lips told me he was pleased with the compliment.

A woman in a service uniform came out of the building in a hurry. She stopped next to Billy and whispered into his ear.

Billy frowned, and shook his head, then gave her the one-moment sign with his finger. He turned back to us. "I have to go, but you folks let me know if you need anything. The concierge desk is open twenty-four-seven."

"Thanks, Billy," Nadine said. "We're just taking everything in today."

Billy turned on his heel and jogged into the hotel.

Nadine turned to Buzz. "So, what was up with those two?"

Buzz arched a brow at her.

Nadine shook her head and smirked. "Don't even act like you didn't hear all that whispering." In a quiet voice, she added. "Shifter One-Oh-One."

He scratched his beard and rolled his eyes.

Nadine thinned her lips. "Just tell me."

Buzz grinned. "The lift motor isn't working, and there are guests stuck halfway up the slope."

"Yikes," she muttered. "That doesn't sound good."

"I'm sure they'll get it fixed right up," Parker said. He looped his arm around my shoulder. "But it might be fun to go check it out."

I gave him a soft elbow to the ribs. "You're so bad." I wiggled my brows. "Let's do it."

"I'm totally in," Nadine quipped before Buzz could protest.

He shook his head but didn't put up any kind of fight. "If watching some stranded tourist dangle precariously from a wire will make you happy...." He spread his hands out.

Ignoring the question in his tone, and without missing a beat, Nadine responded, "It will make me happy."

Buzz chuckled. "Fair enough."

The slopes were down a winding trail packed with chunky gravel and muddy ruts in places where the gravel had worn thin.

"They need to do maintenance on this," Parker observed as he carefully plodded from one rocky patch to another.

There were dog tracks along the narrow path and in the nearby snow. We moved at a quick pace, with Nadine only cussing a few times as the front tire on the triplet's carriage hit every pothole on the way up to the slope. Just past a copse of evergreen trees, the mountain came into view. The lodge was already near the top, so the elevation hadn't been a challenge for any of us.

There was a sign that said all dogs were to be kept leashed and outside the fence.

"We're going to have to watch from here," I said.

"Says you," Nadine told me. "My kids don't need leashes."

"Hah." I smiled. "True story." I reined Smooshie in as she pushed her big head between my knees. Her white paws were caked in mud. "You go have fun. Parker and I will walk down the side of the slope on the fence line for a better view."

Nadine and Buzz went through the gate with the stroller, leaving Parker and me outside.

Eager to check it out, I nudged Parker and said, "Let's go."

He laughed. "You really want to see what's going on, don't you?"

"I really do. I've never seen a ski lift before in real life, and I'm curious." I tugged on Smooshie's leash to get her away from some scent near the bottom of the chain-link. "Come on, girl."

Elvis's leash was slack as he heeled at Parker's side like the goodest boy.

"Take note, Smoosh," I told my loveable goof. "You could learn a thing or two from Elvis's manners."

Parker chuckled. "She shines in her own unique way."

"She sure does." I gave my goodest girl an ear scratch. Smooshie's tail thumped against the back of my thigh. "Let's go," I said again. "Because I really do want to see what's going on before the excitement is over."

There was a short chain-link fence traversing the outer edge of the slope for spectators. About twenty feet inside the fence, an orange woven fence lined the powdery mountain to catch skiers who might take a wild turn on their run.

We saw several empty lifts on a high wire on the far side of the slope but didn't see anyone in them. The stranded guests had to be farther down, closer to the bottom. It started to snow as we made our way down.

"It's really unusual for these ski lifts to break down." Parker tilted his head back as several large snowflakes melted on his face. "Isn't it?"

"I don't know," I told him ominously. "Every movie where skiing is involved, people end up stuck on the lifts."

He smirked. "Name one."

I frowned. "You know I'm terrible with titles...." Then one popped into my head. I snapped my fingers. "*Frozen*."

"The Disney cartoon?"

"Uhm, no. *Frozen* is one of those survival movies. Instead of singing *Let it Go*, everyone was screaming, don't let go."

He quirked a brow at me.

I shook my head. "Think *Open Water* on a ski lift."

He rolled his eyes. "I'm going to let this conversation go."

"Okay, Elsa." I grinned. "You do that."

Distant shouts for help drew our attention. Unfortunately, I couldn't see around the tree line to get a clear view of the lower half of the slope.

As if to prove my earlier point, a woman screamed, "Don't let go."

Holy cow. This was a survival movie come to life.

"That's not good," Parker said.

"Not good at all," I agreed. When she screamed again, I acted on instinct. Without thinking, I handed Smooshie's leash to Parker and jumped the fence.

"Smooshie, no!" I heard Parker shout. "Wait."

Smooshie had gotten away from him. She jumped the fence after me and barreled through the orange mesh. A panel of it gave way and somehow attached itself to Smooshie's head, but it didn't stop my girl. She was hot on my heels, fence section in tow, as I high footed it through the deep snow and I made my way onto the slope.

"Damn it, girl. Go back," I yelled over my shoulder. My fur baby was a total disaster.

Then I saw it. The real disaster. A woman was dangling from the ski lift. The only thing keeping her from dropping to the ground from thirty feet up was a man's grip on her jacket. If he dropped her, I didn't see her surviving without some serious damage to her person.

"Help," she screamed again. "Please, please, please." Those *pleases* were a desperate prayer.

Shoot. I had no idea what to do next. Because I'm a shifter, I can jump higher than humans, but not thirty feet up. Not that jumping would do me any good. I'm also faster and stronger. But I'm also short. The woman dangling had me by at least a few inches. I wasn't sure I could keep her from smashing into the ground, even if I caught her.

"Hang on," I hollered up to her. "I'm here to help."

As soon as I figured out how.

CHAPTER 3

The snowfall had kicked up into a flurry of giant flakes. The man in the ski lift had both hands on the woman's jacket at the shoulders and was furiously blinking away the snow while precariously maintaining his grips.

"She's slipping!" he bellowed. "I can't...."

"Jonathan," the woman said. "Please."

A man geared up from head to toe in skiwear, including solar reflective goggles, appeared. He was dragging a dry bag behind him.

"Hang on, Mrs. Waddle. Get back in the chair if you can," he shouted.

"The front bar snapped," the man gripping her called back. "She's slipping. I can't hold on much longer."

"I'm here to help," the guy announced. He pulled a bundled rope with a weighted end out of the bag. It was tied with a slip knot, but he struggled to get it undone.

Mrs. Waddle screamed, and my heart picked up a

notch as I saw Jonathan holding only her jacket hood as she dropped down a few inches.

Smooshie let out an excited bark.

"Please control your dog," the would-be rescuer said, his voice an octave higher and filled with anxiety as he struggled to untangle his rope.

I glanced over at Smoosh. My poor poopy-potamus had gotten her head stuck between the weave in the orange section she'd demolished.

I rushed to her. The nylon cording that made up the fence was woven like a fishing net, but instead of fish, the dang thing had caught a seventy-five-pound bully. Smooshie's head had gone through the slot easy enough, but she was struggling to back out of the flexible confinement.

The cord was stretched to its max around her neck, and even with my cougar strength, I couldn't simply break the fence to get her out. After all, the barrier was designed to stop large, adult skiers going at top speeds from barreling off the mountain. In other words, it was built tough. Tougher than my precocious pupper.

Smooshie whimpered.

Parker had found a way inside the main fence with Elvis, and they were stridently heading our way. He had his pocketknife out, and I held Smoosh still as he sliced through one of the lines that restrained her, then slid the net from around her neck and over her big head.

Her smile split her giant maw as she licked up the side of my face before she started zooming back and forth. I met Parker's gaze. "Thanks."

"She's slipping," the man on the lift shouted.

The rescuer yelled up, "I'm almost there. I'm going to throw the rope over the line and slide it over to you."

"I can't hold on," Jonathan hollered.

Parker gathered the webbed fence that had almost been Smooshie's undoing. "Get the other side," he told me.

Immediately, I knew where he was going with the idea. "A net." I grabbed the end. "Great idea."

"If it works," he agreed. "Hey, Buddy," Parker barked at the skier with the rope. "Move."

We positioned ourselves under the dangling woman as the man holding her let out a strangled cry. The woman screamed as she plummeted the thirty feet, and I prayed our makeshift safety net protected her from smashing into the ground. Parker and I pulled the webbing as tight as we could. We both leaned back as we held it up, bracing ourselves for her landing. Mrs. Waddle flailed into the center, forcing Parker and me to close the gap. Still, we managed to keep her from smacking into the compacted snow.

Her sobs were the first indication she was all right. We set her down, and I went to her. "Are you okay?" I asked, doing my best to assess her for damage, which was harder than it had to be since Smooshie had jammed her big head under my armpit.

"I...I'm..." Tufts of bright, blonde hair poked out from around the woman's fuzzy ski cap. She looked around as if bewildered. "I'm alive. I can't believe it. I'm okay. Thank you. Thank you so much."

I'd gotten better at guessing human ages since living in Moonrise for the past several years, but I could tell the woman had some work done. Her eyes were a little too tight, her forehead lacked movement, her jowls were lifted, and her lips filled. Still, the work wasn't so crazy that she looked plastic. On the contrary, Mrs. Waddle was an attractive woman.

I smiled and gestured between my guy and my dog. "Parker and Smooshie deserve the kudos." Between Smooshie dragging the fence over here and Parker's quick thinking to use it, they definitely got the credit. "All I did was grab the other side."

She clasped my hand. "And you didn't let go."

"True enough," I admitted.

When Parker was assured that Mrs. Waddle wasn't injured, he went right back into action. "You." He pointed to the skier. "Let's get that rope over the line and get that guy down."

The two of them went into action. Parker threw the weighted end of the rope over the line on the first try. They lowered it down and attached a harness, slid the rope over to the ski lift so that Jonathan could keep it close as they sent it up to him.

"Put your arms through, and situate the loop under your arms," the rescuer instructed. "We'll lower you down." He turned to Parker. "I appreciate your help."

Parker nodded. He wrapped the end of the rope around his waist to act as an anchor, and slowly, they lowered the scared man down to the slope.

When he touched the snow with his feet, he wobbled on unsteady legs. "Trudy," he rasped, stumbling toward Mrs. Waddle. "My love, are you all right?"

"I'm fine, Jonathan," she assured him. "Thanks to

these heroes." She held up her hand, and he helped her to her feet. Trudy looked up at the broken lift. "I don't know what happened. It ground to a halt suddenly, and when I tried to brace myself, the safety bar broke loose."

"That shouldn't have happened," our skier said. He took his goggles off, and young, bright blue eyes stared at the busted equipment. "I'm so sorry, Mrs. Waddle."

"Now, Marshall, I told you to call me Trudy." She batted her fake lashes at him. "It's not your fault."

She was feeling good enough to flirt with the young man, so I wasn't too worried about her physical well-being.

A snowmobile slashed across the slope and came to a halt several feet away from where we were standing. The resort manager, Billy, hopped off the seat and tracked across to us. He lit into the young rescuer. "Damn it, Marshall. The slope was closed. What in the heck were you thinking?" He turned to the shaken couple. "My sincerest apologies, Mr. and Mrs. Waddle," he simpered. "I'll be happy to comp your room for a the rest of your stay."

Trudy gave Billy a shrewd look. "Throw in my birthday dinner tonight, and you have a deal."

Billy nodded. "Of course. It goes without saying."

Trudy smiled. "And this nice couple," she gestured between Parker and me, "will be joining Jonathan and our friends for dinner. You'll cover them too, right?"

"Uhm...Absolutely," he agreed.

"And Marshall, too," she added.

Billy's brow furrowed. "As you like, Mrs. Waddle."

"Oh, I like," she gave Marshall an appraising look, then winked at me. "I like it a lot."

I bit back a laugh. Trudy reminded me of Pearl Dixon, a septuagenarian from back home, who had a sarcastic and horny streak in her, and I found myself really enjoying the flirty older woman.

She grabbed my hand. "You will come to dinner tonight, right? It's in Holton Suite, a private dining room next to the indoor restaurant. We need to celebrate you both saving my life."

"We're with our family," I told her. "We couldn't possibly go out without them. Not on our first night here." We'd planned to cook in the cabin most nights to save some money. "Besides, there are too many of us to accommodate, including three babies."

Trudy shook her head and brushed away my concerns. "The more, the merrier." She glared at Billy. "For my special night, I'm sure we can put a few extra tables together, right?"

Billy winced. "Anything for you, Mrs. Waddle."

"I'm glad we agree."

"I don't think...." I glanced over at Jonathan. The man looked to be a little younger than his wife, but he could just be one of those people who age well. Even so, he was grinning at his wife, and I could see the love.

He looked at me and shrugged. "I learned a long time ago that you don't argue with my Trudy. Not if you don't like losing."

Parker snorted. "Lily doesn't like to lose."

"Then I guess Lily should say yes like it's her idea," Trudy said with a warm smile.

I laughed. "Yes. We'll see you for dinner." Smooshie walked to the end of the leash and squatted as she left a hot trail of yellow across the fine snow.

Billy cringed. "No dogs on the slope."

"Sorry," I offered on Smooshie's behalf. I wrapped her leash around my hand before one last goodbye to the Waddles. "We'll see you tonight."

"Looking forward to it, Lily," Trudy said.

"You know, Trudy, so am I," I replied. And I wasn't lying. There was something about Trudy Waddle that fascinated me. The woman had been dangling thirty feet from an icy death a moment earlier, and now she was asking us out to dinner as if it were the most natural progression after a life-threatening event. I liked that about her. It reminded me of the shifters and witches I grew up with in Paradise Falls. Danger was something that came with being something other than human. If Trudy hadn't been showing some aging, I might have wondered if she didn't have some witch blood.

I smiled, thinking about home, as Parker and I walked the dogs back toward the fence line where the snow was a little deeper and easier to traverse.

I looked back once and saw Billy wave a mittened hand in front of Marshall's face, then pointed to the golden slush. "Get that scooped up before it freezes and someone breaks a neck coming down the hill." To the Waddles, he said, "I'll give you both a ride up the hill on the snowmobile."

Parker chuckled as we hiked back to the top of the

slope. "Was that the kind of excitement you were hoping for?"

I shook my head. "It was a little too close to a survival movie for my taste."

"What did you make of Trudy?" he asked.

"She's smart, funny...." I shrugged. "Clever."

Parker smirked. "You really like her."

"I do," I told him. "You're clever too. Using that webbed fence to act as a safety net was brilliant."

"I can't take too much of the credit," he said. "There was a video of some teens who saved someone dangling from a lift that way a couple of years ago. It had been all over the news at the time, but I forgot all about it until I saw you fighting to get it from around Smooshie's neck."

"Still, it was quick thinking." We were close to the top now. Buzz and Nadine waved their hands to get our attention. I nodded in their direction. "They are going to be bummed they missed all the action."

"I have a feeling Buzz is fine staying out of the limelight."

"True enough," I agreed. Smooshie pulled me to a halt to ram her big nose into the snow. Parker was a few feet ahead of us before he realized we'd stopped. I casually reached down and scooped up a handful of snow, then tugged Smooshie. "Let's go, girl. You can sniff all you want when we get to the cabin."

She barked her excitement at the tone of my words.

We caught up to Parker and Elvis right before we were at the top of the hill, and I slipped my hand under

Parker's coat then rammed the handful of snow down the back of his pants.

He let out a noise of surprise that made me cackle.

"Payback!" I said, "For the one you put down my shirt earlier."

Parker shook his head as he dug the snow from his behind. "You're so getting it."

I grinned at him. "You'll have to catch me first."

CHAPTER 4

The scent of grilled steak and onions dominated the area outside the entrance to Husky's Restaurant. Luckily, there was a sign for *Trudy Waddle's 60th Birthday Celebration* with an arrow pointing the way to the Holton Suite.

"This way," Parker told the group.

I'd tried to brush as much snow as possible from my hair, but most of it had melted, and my thick auburn curls started to turn frizzy. We were all damp from the walk from the parking lot into the main building.

Because of the snowfall, we'd driven to the resort in Buzz's new SUV. Mostly because it was the only vehicle with enough room for all of us to fit. Walking hadn't been an option. The snow was coming down hard, and it would have filled the triplet's stroller. We'd left the dogs back at the cabin. They all got along for the most part, but we put Elvis and Smooshie in our room before we left for dinner to prevent any tension between them and Elinor and Edward. Sometimes rough stuff happened, and we didn't want any of our fur-kids to pay the price for our short-sightedness.

"Are you sure this woman wants three screaming babies at her birthday party?" Nadine asked as she pushed the stroller. None of the kids were screaming. On the contrary, the ride over had put them all in what can only be described as a kiddy coma.

"Those babies are sweet as pie," Reggie protested. She leaned over and tweaked Journey's nose. "Don't listen to your mamma."

Nadine pursed her lips. "They already don't listen to me. I don't think they need any encouragement."

Greer had been quiet since we'd left the cabin.

"Are you okay?" I asked.

He nodded. "It's really coming down out there. The national weather service was calling for light flurries, but it's starting to look more like a blizzard."

I smiled at him. "Then it's a good thing we don't have to be anywhere."

Greer squinted as he glanced back toward the front doors. "I suppose so. Still, I don't like being snowed in."

"Childhood trauma?" I teased.

"Yes," he said bluntly.

His seriousness startled me. "I'm so sorry, Greer. I was only kidding with you. If I had known...."

The corners of his eyes crinkled as he snickered. It was only then that I realized he was messing with me as well. Only, his *Yes* hadn't set off my internal lie detector. It made me wonder why he was reacting so strangely to the snowstorm because there was no doubt that it bothered him. Whatever the cause, he didn't want to talk about it, so I didn't push. Even so, I'll admit I was curious. I'd ask Parker later. If anyone knew why his father was feeling uneasy, it would be him.

The double doors to the Holton Suite were wedged open, and several guests were going inside, including Cat and Dade, the couple we'd met on the road.

"Oh my gosh," Cat exclaimed when she saw me. "Lily! How nice. I had no idea you knew Trudy."

"Hi, Cat," I replied. "Just met her today. How do you know her?"

"She arrived last week when Dade and I got here." She leaned in conspiratorially. "We've become bourbon buddies while our husbands work out in the gym." She winked. "Everyone needs a hobby, am I right?"

She was a gregarious woman, not a shy mouse. That didn't line up with someone who was being abused, but I'd seen with my own eyes how controlling Dade had been. Had I misread the situation?

I smiled at Cat. "Hobbies are good. We better get inside before all the good seats are taken."

She laughed as if I'd told a hilarious joke then went inside the room. I was beginning to think Cat had partaken in her "hobby" before arriving. Only, I didn't smell alcohol on her, and there would be no hiding the acridly sweet scent from my nose.

There were five circular tables dressed in white table cloths and finished with floral centerpieces. Each table had six place settings. Unfortunately, there were no completely empty tables. I pointed to one that had four chairs available. "Why don't you all sit there?" I asked Nadine, Buzz, Reggie, and Greer. "Parker and I will take those." I gestured to a table next to theirs that had two open seats. "We'll still be close, and we can keep the kids between us."

"Sounds like a plan," Buzz said. He had a relaxed smile on his face. He was enjoying himself. I think this was his first real vacation as well. Buzz had spent his entire adulthood spending a decade or less in one place then moving on. Because we were shifters, we aged much more slowly than humans. Buzz, who looked to be in his mid-thirties, was actually nearer to eighty years old. This meant in order to live amongst humans, we couldn't allow ourselves to get attached to people or places. Not if we wanted to stay under the radar. Only, we did form bonds. Thank the goddess.

I squeezed Parker's hand as he pulled the dining chair out for me.

After thirty-odd years of being alone without a mate, I'd believed I was destined to move through this life alone. Parker changed all that for me. And while Buzz might have been in love with my mother once, I knew, soul-deep, he loved Nadine deeper than any mate bond could manufacture. He would do anything to make her happy, and he'd proved it when he forced himself to stay in human form for six months, a hazardous feat for shifters, in order to have a child with her.

Of course, the process involved in-vitro fertilization, which is why they had not one but three children.

Parker kissed my cheek after he scooted my chair in, then took the seat next to me.

"Where's Trudy?" I scanned the room and couldn't find the birthday girl.

"I'm sure she's being fashionably late," a woman next to me said. She had sandy blonde hair, upswept on the sides, held with a pretty sapphire-jeweled clip shaped like a crescent moon. The blue sapphires matched her blue cashmere sweater. "I'm Greta." She smiled. "I don't think we've met."

"Lily," I told her. "And this is my husband, Parker."

"Oh." Her eyes widened for a moment. "The heroes," she said. "Trudy regaled us with tales of your valor."

"Are you related?" I asked.

"My mother-in-law," Greta said. "My husband, Paul, is her son." She gestured to a dark-haired man on the other side of her. He looked to be in his late thirties, early forties. He paid no attention to us as he stared expectantly toward the door before darting his gaze around the room. He was looking for someone. His mother possibly.

I turned my attention back to Greta. "Is it mostly Trudy's family here?"

She scoffed. "Not hardly. Paul is her only child, and she doesn't have any other family but us." She absently touched the clip in her hair. "These are mostly Jonathan's friends and a few of his relatives."

"He's her husband. Doesn't that make them family?" Greer was Parker's father, and that made him my kin.

She glanced at me, and our eyes met briefly before she pivoted her gaze. "I suppose you're right."

"Sit somewhere else," a man spoke sharply. I recognized the voice right away as Dade.

"Dude, what's your damage?" I recognized that voice too. It was Marshall. The young man from the slope.

"If you don't back off my wife, you're going to be the one damaged," Dade snarled.

There were a dozen other people in the room, so it took me a moment to find them. Cat sat at a table on the far side of the room with her back to the wall. The two men were standing in front of the table having their argument. Was Cat's position defensive? As a shifter who'd been in a lot of fights growing up, there was some advantage to knowing you couldn't be attacked from behind. Or was she placed there by her husband so that she couldn't escape?

"That man is a pig," Greta fumed.

I wasn't inclined to disagree with her. I stood up, unsure of what I would do, but I knew I had to do something. Parker put his hand on my arm.

"I'll go with you," he said. Parker wasn't a tall man, but his boxer build gave him gravitas. That, and his military training. "You check on Cat, and I'll take care of her husband."

Billy walked into the suite. "Marshall," he called to the young man. "I need to speak to you for a moment?"

Marshall glared at Dade, then turned and walked away. Or at least, he tried.

Dade Maddox gave a shout of frustration and landed a blow against the back of Marshall's head. The young man careened forward, falling, chest first, onto a nearby table. He grasped at the tablecloth, pulling it with him as he slid off the side. Plates, glasses, and silverware crashed onto the floor. The centerpiece, with its lit candle, followed next, splashing hot wax onto the carpet.

The entire room fell into a shocked silence.

Trudy Waddle, wearing a low-cut, black wrap dress with silver embellishments, entered the room on her husband's arm. Her barking laugh cut through the silence.

She grinned as she took in the scene then nodded. "This," she exclaimed with a flourish of her hand, "is how you kick off a party."

On that note, the lights went out, plunging us into darkness.

There was a collective gasp, then questions, and more than a little outrage from the guests. The candles created pockets of light at each table, but it was still hard to see, even with my enhanced vision.

"Keep calm," Billy said. "It's just a power outage. The generators will kick on in a minute."

There were sounds of people bumping into tables. A man got up from the table in front of mine, and his chair flipped back onto its spine.

"Please stay seated until we get this resolved, for everyone's safety," Billy added when the lights didn't miraculously turn back on. His voice was strained with anxiety. "Just a few more minutes."

There was a thump from somewhere in the back, but when I turned, all I saw was a multitude of shadows on the wall created by the dancing flames.

The lights flickered. There was a quick cheer,

followed by groans when they flickered off again. A woman screamed.

The lights came on again. This time it stuck. I turned to where the scream had come from. Cat Maddox stood at the back of the room. She held a wine glass as she stared in horror at her husband's still body on the floor by her feet. She sipped the wine then set the glass on the table.

Her lips quivered as she stared blankly at the room. "He's dead," she whispered. "Oh my God, he's dead."

CHAPTER 5

Reggie, a general surgeon and a state-certified medical examiner, immediately jumped into action. "Let me through," she instructed the gawpers. "I'm a doctor."

Her authority parted the small crowd without any fanfare. Nadine was out of her chair, as well. "I'm going to need everyone to move out of the room but stay close by."

"Who made you the boss?" someone asked.

"I'm Deputy Sheriff Booth," Nadine answered. "And I am the closest thing you have to law enforcement." She snapped at Billy, who was hovering nearby. "You, call nine-one-one and let the local police know we have a situation."

Billy's voice took on a pinched tone. "Do we really need the police? It was probably an accident. Mr. Maddox does...did like to drink. He could have passed out and hit his head."

I'd watched Dade when he'd arrived. He hadn't been

fall-down drunk. Still, it had been dark, and he could've tripped and hit his head on something.

"Until the police say otherwise, we have to treat his death as suspicious," Nadine told Billy. "Sorry. That's standard."

Reggie assessed the body, then let out a surprised gasp. "He's alive."

Nadine barked at Billy again. "Get an ambulance up here, too. Asap."

The news elicited a swoon from Cat. She staggered back, her fingertips pressed to her chest. I weaved around Parker and Greta, then put my arm around Cat's waist to steady her.

She gave me a weak smile before reaching back and snatching the wine glass from the table. She downed the rest of the drink in one giant gulp. "Is he really alive?" she asked.

"If Reggie says he is, then he is," I told her. Her reaction wasn't what I would expect from a grieving wife, but it had been obvious to anyone paying attention that Cat and Dade had problems. Of course, not everyone handled grief and stress the same way. Drinking herself into a stupor might be Cat's way of dealing.

"He's got a contusion to the back of his head," Reggie said. "A big bump, but no blood, so whatever hit him wasn't sharp." She lifted his eyelids one at a time. Dade's eyes were moving rapidly side-to-side. I recognized it as nystagmus, which can be caused by nerve disorders and other eye problems. Only, I hadn't seen his eyes flicker like that earlier, which meant this was something new.

Reggie covered then uncovered them with her palms. She glanced at Nadine. "His pupils are non-reactive."

"What does that mean?" Cat asked softly.

"It could mean a lot of things," I said gently. Most likely, it meant that his brainstem was damaged, but I'd leave the diagnosing to those more qualified.

There was no blood from the head wound, but I caught the scent of some now that the room had cleared out. Instinct pushed my cougar forward. I kept my glowing eyes covertly turned away from the front door and out of Cat's line of sight as I took in a deep inhalation. There was definitely some blood we weren't seeing. My ears twitched as I heard a slight wheeze from Dade. After a couple of seconds, I heard it again.

I pulled back on my inner beast. "Check his lungs," I said. "He's wheezing."

Reggie didn't bother questioning me. She opened Dade's shirt, put her hand behind his back, then pressed her ear to his chest. "He's barely moving any air," she confirmed. She went up on her knees and brought her hand out from under the man.

It was covered in blood. "Damn it," she said. "Nadine, come help me turn him so I can get a look at his wound."

Nadine got down on the floor with her. I looked at Cat. "You should go wait outside while Dr. Crawford finishes taking care of Dade."

The woman nodded numbly and left.

I lowered myself to my knees near Dade and said, "What do you need me to do?"

"Lily, keep his head between your hands and hold it as steady as you can as Nadine log rolls him toward her. I'll check out the wound." She shook her head, and in a quiet voice, she added, "Between the head injury and the loss of blood, I'm not sure he's going to make it until the ambulance gets here. Even if he does...." Her eyes widened as she examined his back. "He has some kind of laceration about an inch wide, jagged edge, between his fourth and fifth rib on the right side."

"Like he was stabbed?" Nadine asked.

"Exactly like that," Reggie said. "I can't check for depth, but there are bubbles around the blood oozing out. Whatever was thrust into his back definitely punctured the lung."

A gurgling sound emitted from Dade as frothy pink spittle dribbled from his lips. His body began to convulse, and his arms and legs contracted up toward his body.

"I can't hold him still," I told Reggie. "What's happening to him?"

"I honestly don't know." Even though she spoke calmly, her wrinkled brow showed her worry. "A punctured lung could cause the foaming at the mouth, but not this. I think he's having a seizure."

Dade let out a strangled gag before he stopped moving, and the last of his breath left his body.

"He's gone," Reggie said.

"Christ all mighty," Nadine hissed. "In the book of awful, that ranks right at the top."

Unfortunately, it barely scratched the surface of my list of awful, but I agreed, it was pretty terrible.

Reggie kept her voice quiet as she said, "I'm confident this is murder. This man has been bludgeoned in the head and stabbed in the back." She chewed her upper lip, transferring a smear of red lipstick to her teeth. "And if I'm not mistaken, he's been poisoned."

"Poisoned?" Nadine scooted back. "With what?"

"That, I can't tell you," Reggie said. "Until we can find out, we all need to go wash our hands really well, in case we were exposed."

I nodded. "And the body?"

"It can't be moved until the local P.D. arrives," Nadine said. "So, we just lock the door of the suite until they get here."

As we left the room, Nadine closed the door behind us.

"No one goes in there," she instructed.

Greer stayed with the triplets as Buzz and Parker went in stood in front of the door as an extra measure to make sure Nadine's order was followed.

Reggie bee-lined her way to the women's bathroom, located across the lobby. Her hands were covered in blood, and she was anxious to get it off. Nadine and I, though not as urgently, followed after her and washed with soap and water for a good minute.

When we returned to the Holton Suite, Nadine held out her hand to Billy. "You got the keys?"

Billy's face was pale, and he looked as if he would faint as he handed her the keys. "Is he…?"

Nadine nodded. "'Fraid so." She didn't tell him

more. "You can cancel the ambulance. When will the police arrive? We should call and tell them to send the coroner as well."

Billy shook his head. "They're not coming." He scrubbed his face with his palms. "Christ," he muttered. "A semi-truck overturned and took out a transformer, knocking out all the power to the resort, and the snowdrifts have gotten so high, the road up here isn't drivable. Can't get a chopper up here in this weather, either."

Uncharacteristically, Nadine reached out and snatched Billy's wrist and yanked him close. "Are you telling me we don't have power, and there's no way on or off this mountain?"

"I could send Marshall with the snowmobile, but in the dark with the blizzard still going strong...."

"It's too dangerous," I said. "Besides, until we figure out what happened or the local police show up, it's better to keep everyone together."

"Which leads me to my next news," Billy said with apprehension. "I'm afraid all guests will have to move their belongings to the resort, at least until the power is restored. The generators are only good for the main building. The cabins are without power."

"And when will the power come back on?" I asked.

"It's anyone's guess." Billy shrugged. "With the weather the way it is, I don't see the electric company getting someone out to repair the transformer before morning."

My gut twisted. "What about our dogs?"

"You'll have to bring them up here. We are making

rooms available to all our cabin guests. The generators run all the basic functions, including the kitchen. No elevators, though." He plucked his lower lip between his thumb and forefinger. "We just have to find a way to let the cabins know what's going on."

"Can't you call them?" I asked. "Everyone has cell phones now."

"The computers are on a different system. We won't have access until the power comes back, so I don't have those numbers available." He stared at the closed door to the Holton Suite. "I hope everyone can be discreet about Mr. Maddox."

"Dude." Nadine scoffed. "In a perfect world, it's hard to keep something like this from getting out. But we have at least a dozen guests who know someone died. You're not going to be able to keep this quiet. Not unless you plan on locking all these witnesses up for the night."

He gave her a hopeful look. "Can we do that?"

Nadine shook her head. "Nope."

Greer was holding one of the triplets, bouncing the baby in one arm while holding onto the stroller with the other. Buzz left Parker by the door to give the poor guy an assist.

I made my way to Parker. "I have to go to the cabin and get the dogs. We're going to have to bunk in the resort for the night." I filled him in on the power situation. "Doesn't look like they will get electricity other than the generators until tomorrow, and there's not enough fuel to keep all the cabin's going too."

"I'll come with you," Parker said.

"No," I told him quietly. "I'll take Buzz. We're both better equipped to deal with cold weather. It's in our DNA." It's all I was willing to say in mixed company, but Parker got the gist of it. "Besides, you know how he is about his truck. He wouldn't want anyone driving it other than him."

"Okay," Parker conceded. He rested his hands on my shoulders and dipped his head to kiss me. "You be careful, okay."

"I'll be quick. I promise."

He kissed me again. "Holding you to it."

I went to Buzz to appraise him of the plan. "Can you drive me to the cabin? We can pack clothes, toiletries, and the dogs and bring them back here." Buzz could handle choosing items for Nadine. I knew Parker well enough to know what he needed, but I had to ask Greer and Reggie for their list.

"Pajamas, jeans, sweater, shirt, clean underwear from the top two drawers, and everything from the vanity," I repeated back to Reggie.

She nodded emphatically. "When you get to be my age, you need it all."

Greer shook his head. "You're beautiful, darling," he told her.

Reggie rewarded him with a pleased smile. "It's because I have all those products."

I loved how Greer could light up my friend. After a disastrous marriage, Reggie hadn't thought love was in the cards for her. Instead, she moved to Moonrise to get away from the man and focused on getting her daughter CeeCee raised and off to college. Then she'd met Greer.

Greer had been a widow for over a decade. He'd had a great love, and for him, that had been the end of it. Until he'd met Reggie. They were a good-looking couple. Reggie was in her mid-forties and Greer his early fifties, and they both took diligent care of their health. Which meant they had a lot of life to live and love.

"What are you going to do about...Dade?" I asked Reggie.

"I'm going to have to collect evidence tonight. I told Billy I needed the first aid kit for the gloves, and I'll see whatever other items I can utilize. He's also getting me plastic baggies, paper lunch sacks, and a *Sharpie* so I can collect and document whatever I find. Nadine is going to photograph everything." She sucked her teeth, making a tisk sound. "I'm not sure what we're going to do with the body. I just know we can't leave it on the floor in there. The room is too warm, and the decomposition can compromise the body. I'll have to find an exterior room with windows we can crack open." She raised her chin as if having an a-ha moment. "In the top right drawer in the bathroom, Greer has a packet of cotton swabs. Bring those too. I can use them to sample the wound, along with the victim's mouth and nose."

I made a mental note of the extra item. "You got it."

As Buzz and I grabbed our jackets and headed to the exit, Trudy Waddle whistled. "Hey, hero girl. Where you headed off to?"

"To get some clothes and our pups."

She shook her head. "Woo. Mother nature knows how to throw a spectacular party, huh? She's literally showering my day with an abundance of confetti." Her smile was tight. "That poor man," she said. "Awful what happened to him. He fell and hit his head, right?"

I felt the slight itch of deceit. Trudy was hiding something. "Terrible," I agreed. "I really don't know too much. At least, nothing I can talk about."

Trudy frowned. "Well, I'm truly sorry for getting you and your family all mixed up with this mess."

That was the truth. "It's not our first time dealing with trouble."

"With a deputy and a doctor in your fold, I'd say so." She lowered her gaze at me. "We got lucky tonight to be in such good company."

Ding. Ding. Ding.

Trudy's last comment had been a complete lie.

CHAPTER 6

"Watch yourself," Buzz warned as I sunk a booted foot into a snow-covered dip outside our cabin and went down on a knee. The hotel had provided us with a flashlight, and Buzz kept a Maglite in his truck, though as shifters, we didn't need much light to see.

"Too late for that," I told him. The moonlight hitting the snow made it look like we were being attacked by millions of shimmering fireflies. "Wow. It's really coming down out here."

"Sure is." Buzz high-stepped it to the cabin door. He scratched his beard before digging the keys from his jacket pocket. "You know, we've gone an entire year without you tripping over a body. I thought your bad luck streak had ended."

Since my move to Moonrise, I'd developed a reputation as a dead body magnet—a reputation I'd happily give up. "Considering I'm never the body, I'd say my lucky streak was more good than bad."

"True," Buzz unlocked the door. We could hear warning barks on the other side of the door that I knew would turn into happy wags the moment Elinor and Edward knew it was us.

"Still safer than Paradise Falls," I countered.

"You ain't kidding," Buzz replied.

Paradise Falls, where we were originally from, was an entire witch and shifter town. No humans allowed. I'd taken Parker there once for a wedding, and it had turned into a full-on battle. It was the first time I'd seen my guy in action. He'd helped me take down a warlock hellbent on ruining my best friend Hazel's nuptials. Other than a murderous wedding planner and an unfortunate shifter named Gary Gary, who'd been poisoned with currant jam, we'd managed to keep the carnage down to a minimum. However, there had been a few dismemberments that had to be magically healed.

Parker had still loved me when it was all over, thank the goddess, but he wasn't in any hurry to go back for another visit.

Elinor, the smaller of the two dogs, shoved her big head between my knees in greeting when we were inside the cabin. I obliged her with a thorough butt scratch. A few seconds later, she wiggled herself back into the living room area. All the dogs had been fed and given a treat before we'd left for dinner, so I knew they weren't hungry. However, my stomach started to complain. Shifters had a higher core body temperature than humans, so we burned a lot of calories with minimal effort. Nadine and Reggie liked to tease me that I had a hollow leg because I was the smallest of our trio in height and waistline, but I put away twice as much food as the two of them combined.

I went to the fridge and grabbed a bag of smoked sausage sticks I'd put in there for snacks. I took six out and gave Buzz three of them.

"Thanks." He took a bite. "Damn, that's good."

"Got them from that Amish butcher shop that opened up outside Cape Girardeau," I said. "They make the best freaking bacon, too."

He waved a meat stick at me. "I'll have to make a trip."

"Speaking of trips. Do you sometimes miss Paradise Falls? You know, being with our own kind?" I asked him.

He chewed on the meat for a few seconds as if contemplating his response. Finally, he said, "Sometimes."

"You ever think about going back?"

"Never." Buzz shook his head. "I miss not having to hide a part of myself from everyone, but I don't miss all the politics or the fighting and maiming, and I definitely don't miss the witches. Besides, you, Nadine, and the kids, you guys are my kind. Even Parker, Greer, and Reggie. My family." He smiled at me. "Thank you, Lily."

"For what?"

"For finding me. For teaching me that there is more to living than existing. And for showing me that we should be ready and willing to risk everything to be with the people we love."

I teared up at his words but gave his shoulder a playful punch to play it off. "I'm glad I found you, too."

We finished off the last of the sausages in silence,

then Buzz said, "We better get all our stuff and get back up to the lodge."

"Good plan. That's snows not getting any less deep out there."

"Do you think we should do something with the food, so it doesn't go bad?" There were steaks, ground beef, hot dogs, and other meats in the freezer.

"If the power comes on tomorrow, it should be okay. Don't open the door anymore, though."

Since Buzz owned a restaurant, he knew more about food safety than I did, so I took his word for it.

I went upstairs to get the dogs and get our stuff packed up. Smooshie was thrilled to be out of the room, but Elvis was a little more reluctant as he loped down from the bed and gave his back legs a good stretch. I worried about him. He was an older dog, going on eight years, and I noticed he was moving with a little more stiffness these days. I'd gotten an associate's degree at our local community college and graduated with honors as a veterinarian technician. I worked a few hours a week at Petry's Pet Clinic owned by Ryan Petry, a longtime friend of Parker's who'd helped Parker make his pit bull rescue a reality. With my clinical degree, I could bridge the gap between the physical needs and the medical needs of our rescues. I could provide care onsite, under Ryan's supervision, of course. It had made a world of difference in recovery time for our dogs that needed the most support.

"Come here, boy," I said to Elvis. I gave his back and legs a quick massage to help him get going. I didn't like thinking about him getting older, but there was no stopping time. However, I could make his last few years more comfortable. I'd ask Ryan next week about some arthritis medication for him.

Smooshie shoved Elvis aside so she could get her rubs in. I shook my head. "You little jealous boop." Still, I obliged with a quick massage for her as well.

"Hurry up," Buzz hollered from downstairs. "Let's get going."

With as much efficiency as possible, I packed up anything we'd need overnight, then gathered the stuff Greer and Reggie wanted, including the cotton swabs. As a precaution, I put Smooshie and Elvis in their winter gear.

"Elinor and Edward have dog parkas by the door," I told Buzz. "We'll get out of here a lot sooner if you help me get them dressed."

Buzz's expression turned bland. "It's only a couple of minutes up the road, and the truck is heated."

"It's dropped at least ten degrees to below freezing," I said. "If something happens to your truck between here and the resort, I'll feel better knowing the dogs won't freeze."

"Fine," he said. "But nothing is going to stop the 'Burb from making it back to the lodge. That thing is built for ditch-driving."

I laughed. "Fair." His off-road Z71 Suburban SUV was a beast of a truck. With three rows of seating, four-wheel drive, and a large V-8 engine, there wasn't a lot that could stop it. "Even so, better safe than sorry."

"I suppose if it were the babies, I'd feel the same way." He helped me get the Ferrars ready for the blizzard as I filled a reusable grocery bag with snacks and bottled drinks. We took all the bags out to the truck first, then came back for the dogs.

Smooshie whined at the door, pacing back and forth. "Better let them heed the call of nature before we go," I told Buzz.

We got all the dogs on their leashes and took them outside.

Buzz tilted his head back, white crystals gathered in his beard as he squinted up at the quarter moon. "It could be worse," he said. "At least, there's hardly any wind."

He was right. The lack of wind made the night eerily quiet. I held on tightly to Elvis and Smooshie, then tilted my head back and closed my eyes. The snow was cold enough that it wasn't packing, so there was no crunch sounds as the dogs circled around us.

"Do you hear that?" Buzz asked.

"Hear what?" I answered. "Other than the dogs breathing, it's pretty quiet."

"Listen," he said softly.

I nodded and called to my cougar so that I could stretch my hearing. It took a second, but then I found the sound Buzz was trying to identify. A light series of yipping barks. I recognized the tone and cadence because I'd heard it earlier in the day.

"Damn it," I told Buzz. "That's Milo. Cat's dog." His bark was clear enough for me to know that he wasn't inside the cabin. There was no way Cat would've gone back to the cabin after Dade's murder to get him, so there was no reason for him to be loose. Milo's coat was thick and bushy, but his small size would make him vulnerable to the cold weather.

"We can't leave him out here," I told my uncle. "We have to get him."

"Then we better hop to it." Buzz opened the back of his 'Burb, and we got the dogs inside. "Do you remember what cabin they were in?"

"Seven," I told him. "Let's keep an eye out as we go, just in case Milo finds his way to the road."

The windshield wipers dashed back and forth, barely keeping the snow from accumulating on the glass. "We can try. It's hard to see out there."

We were in Cabin 4. Which meant seven had to be three cabins down. Of course, with the power out, none of the places had lights on. Another fifty or so yards, and we found Cabin 7. Buzz turned the truck to face the front. He kept the headlights on for illumination.

The fuzzy, white dog was standing on the porch, his yips and barks more frantic now that someone had arrived. I wasn't sure if he was trying to warn us again or if those barks were a plea for help. It didn't matter. He was getting help whether he wanted it or not.

"I'll get him," I told Buzz. "I don't want him getting spooked and running off. You wait here with the dogs."

"Yep," he said. He didn't have the natural affinity for domestic animals that I did.

Parker called me a dog whisperer. I hoped, in Milo's case, it would hold true.

I got out of the truck. "It's okay, Milo. You're safe," I cooed. The little dog backed up. "No, no," I told him. "Stay put. I'll get you nice and warm."

Milo tentatively took a step forward. Good. He was trying to figure out if he could trust me or not, and I planned to show him he could. "What are you doing outside, boy?"

I couldn't imagine Cat leaving him out like this. I could tell earlier that she really loved the dog. "I'm going to take you to your mamma. You'd like that, wouldn't you."

Milo began to whimper. He still wasn't sure if he could trust me, but he was scared and cold, so he was willing to chance it. I was inches away from putting my hand on him when Smooshie began barking, and Milo turned and ran...right into the cabin. The door had been shadowed, but now I could see it was standing wide open.

Strange. I pulled out my phone and used the flashlight app to examine the door. The keyhole was damaged, and there were scrapes on the gatehouse plate. Wooden splinters from where the door had been forced were on the floor.

Buzz lowered his window and shouted, "What's going on?"

"Nothing good," I told him. I closed the door to keep Milo inside as I went to talk to Buzz. "It looks like while Dade was being murdered, someone broke into the cabin."

"Damn," he said.

"Yep," I agreed. "Double damn."

CHAPTER 7

The moment I stepped into the cabin, I realized that whoever might have broken in could still be here. Buzz must've had the same idea because he was suddenly behind me in the doorway.

"I'll clear the bedroom and the bathroom," I told him in a hushed voice. "You take the kitchen and the living room. Check the back door, too."

"Got it," he responded.

The layout was much like our cabin. Only the second story had been left out. Without the staircase, they had more open space between the living and dining rooms. Our cabin had a half bath on the lower floor as well, but this one only had the master bathroom. The benefit again had been more space. Cabin 7 had a whirlpool tub and a large separate shower.

"The backdoor is unlocked," Buzz hollered. "I see tracks on the deck, but then they disappear. They have to be fresh, though, because the snow is filling in the depressions quickly."

So, the person had broken in through the front door and then left through the back. Why? Had they gotten spooked? "You think the thief was here when we arrived?"

"It's a good possibility," Buzz replied.

In the bedroom, the closet was open, and clothes were off the hangers. I checked the laptop bag near the queen-sized bed, and there was a computer and tablet inside. A dish with some jewelry in it, and a box that contained what looked to be an expensive watch that made a distinctive ticking sound, sat on top of the dresser. All three top drawers had been pulled out, and there were underwear and socks, along with a lacy corset thrown on the ground. Had the Maddox's been in a hurry? Maybe. I'd ask Cat. If they hadn't done this, then whoever had broken in was looking for something specific. A thief would have grabbed the laptop and the watch. I found a prescription nasal spray inside the bedside table drawer next to a Gideons Bible. The pharmacological name was *esketamine,* and it was labeled for depression. The name on the prescription label was Catherine Maddox. I hadn't heard of a nasal spray drug to treat depression, but my drug book was decades old. I'd look it up later.

I listened to the anxiety-laden pants of Milo. I'd heard him breathing when I came into the bedroom, so I knew he'd been hiding under the bed. On the side closest to the door was a soft crate for a small dog. I unzipped the front and faced the opening at the bed.

After, I got down on my stomach and peeked under the frame. "Hey, fella," I said calmly. "I see you found yourself a nice place to hide." I kept treats in my coat pockets for when I caught Smooshie being good, so I took one out and slid it to the scared pup. "You chew on that for a minute, okay?"

Milo's belly overrode his fear, and he snapped up the tiny bone-shaped biscuit. I smiled. I was often ruled by my stomach as well, so I couldn't fault him. I rolled onto my side and lay still, allowing him to get used to my presence.

That's when I saw it. A large white envelope had been tucked between the wooden support slats and the box spring. "You're such a smart boy, Milo," I told the dog. "You knew the best hiding spot, didn't you?"

I didn't immediately get up to retrieve my discovery. I didn't want to weaken the trust I was building with the dog. Instead, I got another treat out. I placed it at the end of my reach, then pulled my hand back but left it close to my fingertips. After a moment's hesitation, Milo crawled toward me and ate the snack. I used one more snack to keep in my palm. I wouldn't normally use bribery to get a dog to trust me. However, these were extraordinary circumstances, and Milo took the bait. He ate the last snack out of my palm then licked my fingers. I sat up then scooted back from the bed. Milo followed me out from under the mattress, and I was grateful I hadn't had to drag him out.

I was out of snacks, so I pretended to toss one into the crate. Poor Milo fell for it. "Sorry, dude," I told him as I zipped him in. "I'll owe you one."

Buzz came into the bedroom. "I see you found the dog."

I wiggled my brows. "That's not all." I walked to the other side of the bed and lifted the box spring. I snatched up the envelope and held it up. "I also found this."

His lips thinned with mild exasperation. "And what exactly is *this*?"

I frowned at his lack of enthusiasm. "It's a large bubble mailer of secrets," I replied, then added a "Duh" at the end.

Buzz sighed. "Why is it under the mattress?"

"That's the exact right question." I pulled the tab to unseal the envelope. "Let's find out."

"Is this legal?"

I wrinkled my nose at him. "Probably not. Though, we're not the law, so...."

"So, we can get charged with breaking and entering if we get caught."

"Technically, only entering." This wasn't the first time Buzz had helped me search a dead guy's place, but I was betting this packet contained more than pictures of a secret love child. "Look," I added. "It's already open, so we might as well take a peek."

"Because you opened it," Buzz said.

"True, but it's too late now." I slid my fingers into the crack and widened the opening.

"What's in there?"

"Oh, now you want to know?"

"I never *not* wanted to know."

"You just wanted deniability with Nadine, huh?"

He smirked. "Pretty much. She doesn't get as mad at you as she does me."

"Because she loves you more," I said. "It makes disappointment that much harder to bear." I shrugged. "Besides, I'm adorable. No one can stay mad at me."

He laughed. "I think Parker's been really good for you, Lily. You're not the same serious woman who arrived in Moonrise."

"Trust me," I said. "She's still in there."

But he wasn't wrong. I had changed. Since my handfast marriage to Parker, I'd felt lighter. More carefree. My husband made me feel safe. Made me feel like I had a home. It was something I hadn't felt, not completely since my parents were murdered when I was seventeen. I had my friend Hazel to thank. She'd arranged for me to find Buzz, my only living relative, and that arrangement had led me to my destined mate.

"So," Buzz prodded. "Are you going to tell me what's in the envelope?"

"It looks like photographs." I emptied the contents onto the bed. I swallowed at the knot forming in my throat. "Oh, wow."

Buzz came around and looked. "Yep," he agreed. "That's pretty wow."

The pictures were compromising shots of Greta doing a lot of naked kissing and more with Billy, the resort manager. They had been printed on regular printer paper, and the odd sizing made me think they had been taken with a phone camera.

"This is a new development I did not see coming," I said with a wince.

"Who's the woman?" Buzz asked. "She was sitting next to you at the party, right?"

I nodded. "She's the birthday girl's daughter-in-law."

"Do you think Maddox was blackmailing her?"

"Or Billy," I said. "It gives them a motive."

Buzz whistled. "It sure does. If that's what the person who broke in was after, we should give the packet to Nadine." He shook his head. "Stupid cheating like that. Secrets don't like to stay hidden for long."

"Agreed." I pointed to the crated dog. "Let's grab Milo and get going."

GETTING BACK TO THE LODGE HAD BEEN AN adventure. Elinor, who was normally fairly calm, could not keep her nose off Milo's soft crate. The small dog barked incessantly. Buzz's grip on the steering wheel got tighter with each sharp noise. I climbed in the back to keep the dogs calm. Elvis had laid down on the floor behind the front seats, and Smooshie was in the back with me, but she was surprisingly subdued. That is until Buzz slammed on his brakes.

The SUV skidded sideways to a halt as the dogs and I were knocked against the back of the back seat.

I put my arms around Smooshie as she began to tremble. Elinor and Edward huddled together, and I reached over the seat to put my hand on Elvis as he stood up to shake himself off. "What the hell, Buzz?" I snapped. "What happened?"

"Somebody was in the middle of the road," he said, sounding stunned. "He just...he was just there."

"Did you hit him?" I asked.

Buzz shook his head. "I don't think so. I think I missed him."

I climbed over the back seat to the second-row passenger side door.

"What are you doing?"

"I'm going to go see if I can find the guy and make sure he's okay," I grumbled. "You figure out if the truck is stuck or not."

"Fine," Buzz said. "But stay close. It's hard to see out there."

I opened the door. Unfortunately, the wind had started to pick up, and the frigid breeze bit at my face and my ears. With caution, I walked around the back of the 'Burb, then tracked down the road where the skid marks started. If the guy's jacket hadn't been a bright yellow, I would have missed him. Or rather tripped over him, considering he was face down in the snow.

I moved quickly, turning the body over. The guy wore a face mask and goggles, and had on a ski parka, ski pants, and thick gloves. All of this meant it was hard to check for a pulse. I pulled the goggles up, along with the mask, and grunted in surprise.

The man lying on the road was Marshall, the young ski instructor who'd had the altercation with Dade. Why was he out in this weather? Had he been the person who'd broken into the Maddox cabin? Was he out here for another reason?

Before I could check for a pulse, he opened his eyes. They widened for a moment before he rasped out, "Help me."

"Can you get up?" I asked Marshall.

"I think my wrist is broken," he replied.

"How in the world did you do that? And why are you out here on foot?"

"I was on the snowmobile, but it was hard to see. I hit something." He shook his head as I helped him sit up. "I don't know. It could have been a rock or a stump that was hidden by a snowdrift."

"That doesn't answer the question as to why you're out here."

"Billy told me to do a door-to-door knock and check on the cabins and let them know they could move up to the lodge until the power issue gets fixed." He winced as I helped him get to a standing position. "He doesn't want to get sued if anyone freezes to death."

What he said rang primarily true, but like with Trudy, it felt like he was hiding something more. Maybe because he'd been the one who had broken into the Maddox cabin.

"Did you go to Cabin 7?" I asked.

Marshall shook his head. "I only made it to Cabin 3 before I wrecked."

Again, there was a marker of deceit, but not an outright lie. Was my magic off-kilter? Maybe the blizzard was affecting more than the roads.

CHAPTER 8

Buzz and I had managed to get the dogs, our packed items, and Marshall back to the lodge in one piece.

"I just wanted a nice vacation. Get a little skiing in. Play with the dogs. Play with the husband." I wiggled my brows at Nadine and Reggie. "Is that too much to ask?"

"For Moonrise's murder magnet," Nadine said. "Probably."

"You and Buzz need to cut it out with the magnet thing."

Nadine giggled. "Remember the dead body you found in your living room wall?"

The memory of the moment I realized my fixer-upper had several buried secrets played in my head. "How could I forget? I had to chase Smooshie down before she could bury a dried up human foot." I sighed. "And before that, there was poor Katherine Kapersky, dead in Parker's back yard. Strangled to death."

"There was nothing poor about Katherine. She was a real piece of work." Nadine snapped her fingers at me. "Oh, what about Jordan Deeter's mother! I mean, that was just beyond-beyond."

"True that," I told her. "I still can't believe she'd kept her mother's corpse in a sealed bedroom for two weeks."

Nadine's nostrils flared. "Yeah, beyond icky."

"I don't think I could smell vinegar without gagging for nearly a year."

"And then the cut-up guy in the basement of that house."

"Shut up," I said with a laugh. Not because it was funny, but because I had to laugh sometimes or all the horror would overwhelm me. "That one can't be blamed on me. It was outside of town, and technically, I'm not the one who found him."

"Both of you shut up," Reggie said. "You're raising Marshall's blood pressure."

Marshall, whose last name turned out to be Riley, was ghostly pale as Reggie finished splinting and wrapping his wrist. The ski resort, it turned out, had a well-stocked first aid room. It made sense, given the number of ski accidents that had to happen each year. There was even a small refrigerator that Reggie could store evidence samples in until they could be analyzed. Buzz, Greer, and Parker took charge of the human and fur babies. They went off to get keys for our assigned rooms and get the dogs settled while Nadine helped me escort Marshall to the first aid room.

Parker had said he'd make sure Milo was handed off to Cat, too.

Nadine and I stayed with Reggie. She had examined Marshall's wrist and determined there were no obvious breaks, but she couldn't be sure without a film of the injury.

"There," Reggie told him. "It'll get you around. And lucky for you, this place has a sling for your arm. You'll need to wear it for a few days to keep it elevated and reduce swelling. If you can get to town tomorrow, you should go to the hospital for an x-ray, though, just to make sure you don't have a fracture."

"Thanks, Dr. Crawford." Marshall, who looked to be about twenty or twenty-one, ran his fingers through his ear-length brown curls. His hazel eyes were a combination of blue, gray, and gold, and he had pouty lips that I was certain made many a girl swoon. He glanced over and met my gaze. "What was the vinegar for?"

"To cover the smell of decomposition," Nadine told him before I could.

I made a gagging sound. "It was pretty disgusting. And technically, I didn't find that body either. I was hit over the head and placed in there with it by her grieving daughter."

Nadine nodded. "Grieving or not, I'm pretty sure she was planning on offing you next."

I shrugged. "It's too bad about Jordan. She was a good volunteer at the rescue."

"She killed Jock," Reggie said. "No amount of grief excuses murder."

Jock Simmons had been a horrible, horrible man. His actions had led to nothing but misery for so many people, including his widow, Theresa, who happened to be a good friend and Parker's right hand at the pit bull rescue. I was sorry he was murdered, but I couldn't say I was sorry he was gone. I raised my hands, cocked my head to the side, and said, "Eh...."

"Lily!" Reggie's exclamation was a mixture of admonishment and amusement. None of us had grieved Jock's passing.

"Good riddance," Nadine said. "I still can't believe the sheriff tried to pin it on Buzz."

"Buzz is your husband?" Marshall asked Nadine.

"Close enough," she replied with a *move on* tone. She'd told me a few times that Buzz had said he'd marry her if she wanted, and she felt like, if that's the best he could do by way of a proposal, then she was satisfied to keep going the way they were going. I thought about talking to Buzz but figured it was their business to sort out.

Nadine changed the subject by switching into cop mode. "Marshall, can you tell us again what you were doing out there? I specifically told everyone to stay at the lodge."

"Billy was worried about the people in the cabins. He couldn't locate any of the guests from cabins two and five, and he wanted me to double-check the other cabins to make sure no one had stayed in. He's got enough problems."

"What do you mean by that?" I asked.

Marshall sat up on the edge of the exam table, wincing as he dangled his legs over the side. "I don't know. It's something he said."

His answer didn't set off my lie detector.

"Did you see anyone out there on the road or anywhere else when you were driving around?" I asked.

He seemed to chew on the answer for a moment, then said, "No, but it was hard to see anything out there in that storm."

Partial truth.

"Did you see anything moving around out there?" I asked more directly.

"I saw something or someone moving quickly toward the lodge, but I couldn't tell if it was a person or not. It was too fast for anyone on foot, but I was on the snowmobile, so it was hard to hear if another motor was going."

"Is there another snowmobile at the resort?" Nadine asked.

"Yes," Marshall admitted. "But Billy is the only one with keys."

"Please, don't tell him I said anything. I need this job."

"Did he tell you not to talk to us?" I asked.

"Yes," Marshall said, then he looked really surprised at his answer. "I mean, he said to wait until the real police showed up and that we shouldn't stir up any trouble if we could help it."

"Unless we need to, we won't say a word," Nadine assured him.

Hmm. Billy was looking more and more like a killer to me. If Billy was trying to stop people from talking to us, that put another tick in his suspect box, and he was already at the top of the list because of the illicit photos of Greta and him.

Still, we couldn't count Marshall out. After all, Dade had been jealous of Marshall's attention toward Cat, whether it was real or not. Then Dade humiliated Marshall at the party. I was curious about his take on the deceased. "How well did you know Dade Maddox?"

He scrubbed his face. "Not well. He and his wife checked in last week. She's taken a few ski lessons from me. He treats her like she's property. She's a person, damn it." Anxiety lines gathered between his brows. "I mean, no one deserves to be treated like they don't matter."

"I agree." I put my hand on his shoulder. "How are you feeling?"

"Like an idiot who wrecked a snowmobile." He gave me a crooked half-smile, that I had to admit, was quite charming. "Can I go?"

I was certain he used his good looks and affable demeanor to get himself out of a lot of tense situations. But there was only one guy that caught my fancy, and it wasn't Marshall. Of course, there was no reason to keep him here.

"You should go get ice on that wrist," Reggie said. "Ten to fifteen minutes every two hours for the next two days, then you can switch between ice and heat as you need it. Confirmed by a clean x-ray, that is."

Marshall gave her a two-finger salute. "Thanks, Doc."

We watched him cradle his arm as he left the first aid room, and for the first time since Dade died, we were finally together and alone. "So, what did you two find out?" I asked.

"First," Reggie said. "Nadine found the weapon used to stab Maddox."

"Wow." I whistled. "Nice. What was it?"

"A butter knife, dull as can be," Nadine said. "I found it in one of the dirty dish tubs along the wall. Unfortunately, anyone could've thrown it there on the way out. We can't fingerprint it until the local police can get up here with a forensic kit. It might not even have prints on it. I didn't want to mess with it to see and possibly ruin evidence in the process."

"Did any of the tables have a missing butter knife?"

"Nope," Nadine said. "Not a single one."

"Maybe it got brought in from the restaurant," I mused.

Nadine shrugged. "Your guess is as good as anything I've got." She sighed noisily. "I feel like I'm investigating with one hand tied behind my back."

"If anyone is up to the challenge, it's you," I told her. "Plus, you have us, so it's like having four more extra hands. "I looked at Reggie. "What else?"

"I think the man was killed in stages," Reggie replied.

My mouth dropped open. "What do you mean by that?"

Reggie crossed the room and grabbed a clipboard

that had her notes on it. "The contusion on the back of his head, once I removed the hair covering it, was a dark purple, almost black. That puts it at one to two days old. I think it caused an internal hematoma that cut off blood to parts of his brain. I think that's why his pupils were fixed. If I had my equipment here, I'd do an autopsy, but without one, it's only speculation."

"You said stages," I said. "What else?"

"Between the seizure and the rapid eye movement, I think he was dosed with some kind of drug."

"Like what?"

"Carbamazepine, opioids, benzodiazepines, barbiturates...." She let out a noise of frustration. "The list is too long. But an overdose of any of them could be lethal. There's no way of telling, though, until I can send samples off to a lab."

"Barbiturates?" Nadine asked. "Isn't that a sixties drug?"

"It's an anesthetic used for euthanasia," I said. "Like Secobarbital, the barbiturate they use with animals when it's there time to cross the rainbow bridge," I added. I'd studied pet pharmacology in school, and I'd assisted Ryan with a rainbow crossing once. It was one of the hardest things I'd done in a long time. I was glad he hadn't asked me to help again. I knew it was necessary and merciful, but it reminded me of how fragile Smooshie's life was and how, eventually, I would have to say goodbye to her.

"Exactly right," Reggie said. "But it's also used for humans. It's one of the compounds in a lethal injection. And it's sometimes used with physician-assisted suicides." She let out a slow breath. "It's not legal in Missouri, but that doesn't mean people don't find a workaround."

"And why did those drugs pop into your head?" Nadine asked.

"I found some blisters in his mouth and nose, and I read a case study recently that talked about rash and blisters from barbiturates. It made me think of it. Maddox was still alert when he arrived at the party, but it didn't take long for him to succumb to respiratory failure." She rubbed her arms as if to ward off a chill. "Which brings me to the final stage of his murder, the stabbing. Someone jabbed something into his back hard enough to create a sucking chest wound. The blood was fresh, so the stabbing had to have happened seconds before the lights came back on. If that had been his only issue, he could've survived," Reggie said. "But he just stopped breathing."

Nadine whistled. "Cripes. That's some real overkill going on there."

"Maybe whoever hit him wanted to make sure they finished the job," I surmised.

Reggie nodded. "The head injury could've been an accident. He might have hit his head and not even realized how bad it was until it was too late. Whatever happened there, I can say with some certainty, it probably would have been the cause of his death sooner or later."

Nadine swore under her breath, then said, "Well, damn. If the killer would've waited a little while longer...."

Reggie's lips thinned. "Yep, they wouldn't have had to resort to murder."

"Well..." I withdrew the envelope with the photos I'd kept in my jacket and handed it over to Nadine. "I found out a few things too."

CHAPTER 9

"Greta Michaels is having an affair with Billy?" Nadine made a face. "Ew. Not that Billy is gross or anything, but she's out there clinging to her husband's arm like a lifeline right now."

"Do you think he knows?" I asked.

"Your guess is as good as mine. I'd like to say that you always know when your partner is cheating, but I don't think that's true," Nadine answered.

Reggie leaned against the exam table. "I didn't know my husband was cheating on me for the longest time. Only in the last couple of years, when he'd started acting like I didn't exist, did I get a clue. Some people are better liars than others."

Nadine crossed the room and stood next to Reggie. She didn't try to console her, though. There was no need. Reggie was one hundred percent over her ex. The bastard had done her a favor by giving her a legitimate reason to get out of the marriage.

"It's a good thing that we brought our living lie

detector with us then," Nadine told her. "Lily will help us get to the truth."

"If the truth wants to be got," I said. If someone had a secret they honestly didn't want anyone to know, no amount of magic would get them to confess. "Did you interview everyone at the party?"

"Most of them. I still have Trudy and Jonathan Waddle and, of course, the surprisingly stoic bride. She's acting really disconnected." Nadine's shoulders dropped, a testament to her exhaustion. "I hope Buzz is getting the kids settled okay. Jackson can get a little fussy if you don't bounce him. He's the only one of the three that doesn't like to be rocked."

"I'm sure Buzz will remember," I told her. "Why don't you do those last interviews in the morning?"

"That's the plan," Nadine said. "I contacted local law enforcement, and they've granted me privileges to act on their behalf until they can get out here."

"This whole night has been a mess. If I hadn't stuck my nose into that chairlift disaster earlier, we would be in our cabin, eating dinner and going to bed. No muss. No fuss."

Reggie snickered. "You sure are giving yourself a lot of credit for Maddox's murder, a guy so nice they had to murder him thrice."

Nadine snorted. "Please tell me you haven't been sitting on that one all night."

Reggie pushed a loose strand of her black hair back behind her ear. "I might have come up with it earlier when I was doing a more thorough exam."

"You're awful," I said.

Her voice hitched up an octave. "I know."

"And besides," Nadine said. "If you and Parker hadn't gotten to the ski lift when you did, Trudy wouldn't have survived to her sixtieth birthday party."

"I guess..."

"And," Reggie added. "Dade's murder didn't take out the power. We would have still had to deal with a blizzard and no heat."

"Fine." I sighed and threw up my hands. "Did anyone say they saw anything?"

"Like someone poisoning or stabbing the victim?" Nadine asked.

"Something like that."

"Nope." Nadine pushed away from the exam table and started pacing. "They all said they were distracted by the blackout. It was dark. Blah, blah, blah."

"You're the supernatural sleuth," Reggie said. "Did you see anything that shouldn't have been going down?"

"I was distracted by the blackout. It was dark. Blah, blah, blah," I answered. "Sorry. I'm about as useless as the rest of the witnesses. I still can't believe how fast it all happened. It only took about a minute for the power to come back on."

Reggie tapped her watch. "A minute was all our killer needed."

I LEFT THE FIRST AID ROOM READY TO FIND PARKER and our bed. I'd been so excited about this weekend vacation and all its possibilities. Growing up the way I did, the luxury of *getting away* wasn't an option. I worked two jobs, barely making ends meet, from the time I was seventeen years old until I left Paradise Falls seventeen years later. I had done the best I could without any help from my own community of shifters. Being in Moonrise with Parker and all our friends showed me for the first time what could've been if I'd had any support. They always rallied around me when I needed their help, whether it was renovating my home, giving me time to finish my college degree or solving a murder.

I tried not to think about how having real friends and family might have changed my brother's life, as well. It wasn't healthy to rake up the past, not when there was nothing you could do to change it.

"Thank you, Lily," Cat Maddox gushed as she rushed over to me. She clutched Milo to her chest. Her mascara was smeared under her eyes, giving her the appearance of bruising. "I'm so grateful to you for saving my baby."

I gave Milo a scritch between the ears. "He was very brave."

"Oh." She made a cutesy face at her dog. "He really likes you. Milo hates everyone but me, usually."

"It's hard being little in a big world." I knew this from experience.

She patted Milo's back. "Well, I just wanted to make sure I thanked you."

"How are you doing?" I asked. "I'm so sorry for your loss."

Her gaze pivoted away from mine then back. "Yeah,

terrible about Dade. I can't believe it. I'm still in shock."

"I can imagine. If something happened to Parker, I don't know what I'd do."

Cat bobbed her head in agreement. "That's just it, isn't it? I have no idea what's next for me now."

"What did Dade do for a living?" I asked. It was hard not to wonder about, as Reggie put it, a guy so nice you had to kill him thrice.

"He was an investigator," she replied.

That was a turn I didn't see coming. "He was a police officer?"

"No, no," Cat denied with a flourish of her hand. The corridor was brightly lit, but her pupils were large, as she said, "He was an investigator for a law firm in Albuquerque."

"Criminal or civil?" Cat gave me a blank look, so I clarified, "Did he investigate criminal cases, like fraud or civil cases, like lawsuits and such."

"I think both, but he didn't want me in his business, so he didn't talk about it too much. He kept his work private."

A slight itch played over my skin. Cat wasn't being completely truthful, but was it about Dade's job or her lack of knowledge? I wanted to ask her about the break-in, but Nadine hadn't had a chance to talk to her yet, so I didn't. It was an "element of surprise" that could be effective when questioning a suspect, and whether Cat seemed harmless or not, she was a suspect.

"I better go," Cat said. She reached out and touched my forearm. "Thank you again, Lily."

"You're welcome." I noticed as she withdrew her hand that she had a suspiciously straight, vertical scar on her right wrist. It was slightly puckered and faintly pink. Less than a year old.

I took hold of her hand before she could completely retreat. "It was my pleasure," I said, turning the wrist for a better look. The wound was too neat, the edges too tidy for this to be an accident. Cat had tried, at some point over the last year, to commit suicide. "If you need anything, you let me know. Even if it's just to talk."

She must've caught me looking because she pulled her hand away and used Milo to cover the scar. Her frown suddenly turned to a smile. "I better go get this boy settled in for the night. He's had an awful fright."

"Good idea." I forced a smile that couldn't quite match hers. I wasn't nearly as good at faking it. "Good night, Cat." I gave Milo another head scratch. His little tail wagged. "Goodnight to you too."

As she walked away, Cat hummed a happy little ditty that gave me the total creeps.

A poke at my shoulder made me jump.

"Hey," Parker said, holding up his hands as I rounded on him.

I lowered my arms. "You shouldn't sneak up on a jumpy shifter."

"I shouldn't be able to sneak up on a shifter at all," he responded.

I giggled as I melted against his chest. "Don't tell anyone, or they might pull my membership card."

He wrapped his warm arms around me, and I got

lost for a few seconds listening to the steady beat of his heart.

"I got us a room with two double beds," he said. "One for the dogs and one for us."

I chuckled then tilted my head back to look at him. "You think they are going to let us get away with that?"

"We'll just wait for them to choose a bed, then we'll take the other."

"Hah. The minute we choose the other, they will join us in that one."

"Then I guess we're left with shower sex."

A real laugh escaped me then. "I'm good with that." My belly grumbled in sharp protest. "But I need to get some food in me first, or my stomach is going to eat me from the inside out."

He dipped his head and kissed me with such tenderness I swooned. "We can't have that," he said. "Let's get you some dinner."

"Then shower sex for dessert," I told him.

He grinned. "That's definitely on the menu."

I held Parker's hand as we walked down the hall toward the lobby. It was going on nine o'clock. "Is the restaurant still open?"

"No," he said. "But the bar has a burger menu."

"Oh, good." I leaned my head against his shoulder. "Let's get the food to go."

"Works for me." He brought my hand to his lips and gave it a kiss.

Goddess, this man made my heart sing. "Thank you for loving me."

"Loving you is the easiest thing I've ever done in my

entire life." He met my gaze, his expression serious and sincere. "That includes breathing."

Suddenly, I wasn't so hungry. I stopped walking, turned in his arms then raised up onto my tiptoes. I interlocked my fingers behind his neck and said, "We can order room service later. Dessert first."

He tilted his head to the side and gave me a crooked grin. "I've always been a fan of dessert first."

CHAPTER 10

At two a.m., Smooshie planted her paws right into the middle of my stomach. The rush of breath leaving my body woke me up. My sweet yet annoying boop shoved her wet nose against my neck and whined.

"I got it," I told her. "You need to go." I crawled out of bed, trying not to disturb Parker, but that ship had sailed.

He sat up. "I'll go with," he said. "Elvis could use a leg stretch as well."

We got dressed and put on all our winter gear. There was no telling what we'd be walking out into at this time of the night. "Do you think the blizzard is still going on?"

He pulled back the curtain of the room. We were on the first floor, with a clear view of the parking lot. "It looks like it's still snowing, but not as heavy as earlier. The drifts are pretty deep, though."

I put Smooshie in her winter gear while Parker took care of Elvis. "The curse of being a short-haired pooch,"

I told Smooshie. She didn't complain. She knew that putting on the vest meant going on an adventure. Elvis, who was less enthusiastic, tolerated the quilted layers.

"When do you think they'll get the power restored?" I mused.

"No telling. I guess it'll depend on how early they can get the roads cleared in the morning."

"I can't believe we're stuck on this mountain with no way off."

"We weren't planning on leaving until Monday, anyhow," Parker said.

"Yeah, but it's not the same. There's a difference between choosing to be somewhere and being stuck there."

"That's very true." He put his arm around me as we led the dogs through the hall toward a side door that was marked as a doggy-doo area.

The pet retreat was a little fenced-in playground that had two waste stations complete with bags on a roll for everyone's convenience. Because of the blizzard, the play area was two feet deep in snow, with higher drifts up against the fence and the lodge wall.

The wind had picked up and was blowing the frozen flecks around.

"Damn, it's cold," Parker huffed, his escaping breath a foggy cloud.

While I didn't get cold as quickly as humans, this weather was testing even my resilience. "Come on," I told the dogs. "Do your thing, and let's go."

Smooshie barked as she jumped around in the accumulated snow like a bull with a rider on its back. Elvis, with a lot more dignity, walked over to a wall drift, hiked his leg, peed, then went and stood in front of the door.

"He's had enough," I told Parker. I worried the cold was making his arthritis worse. And until the fun of the cold snow wore off for my girl, she wasn't going to settle down enough to do her business. "Go ahead and take him back to the room. Smoosh, and I will be along soon."

"You sure?" he asked. "We can wait for you."

"Nope. You go on back and keep those sheets warm for us." I gave him a quick kiss. "It won't take too long, but you know how she can get."

"She's a pistol," he agreed.

I smiled because the phrase was something his dad said often, and I thought it was adorable that he was only in his late twenties saying things like "she's a pistol." Thinking about Greer, I remembered his earlier uneasiness when he was talking about the blizzard.

I grabbed Parker's arm before he could go. "Is there something going on with Greer?"

"What do you mean?"

"Earlier, before the party, that wasn't a party. He was acting strange about the weather. When I asked him about it, he made a joke, but it felt like something more serious was going on."

"Oh, that." Parker nodded. "It's something that happened when he was a teenager. He and a few buddies got lost in a winter storm. They all made it out after four hours with some frostbite, except for one of them. The guy had panicked and taken off on his own.

Got himself lost. They found him the next day huddled up and frozen near a tree less than half a mile from safety."

"He doesn't blame himself, does he?"

"No, but I think there's always that little bit of survivor's guilt when you make it out of something scary, but a friend doesn't." I caught the haunted look in Parker's eyes. Elvis could feel it. He put his head under Parker's hand. Parker blinked at me. "I'm okay," he said. He gave me a squeeze. "I'll see you back inside."

Smooshie yipped excitedly and dashed around after Elvis and Parker went back inside. Chest deep in snow, she started zooming back and forth. "You are such a goofus," I told her.

In response, Smooshie bolted out to the edge of the fence then dove headfirst into a four-foot drift of pillowy snow. She rolled around, making pit bull angels, then snapped her jaws, biting at the giant flakes stirring up around her.

"It's a good thing you don't have balls," I said. "Or you'd be freezing them off." As it was, my lady balls were like, damn, it's cold. I wished I could shift into my cougar form. Because, honestly, I'd be warmer, and Smooshie looked like she was having a hell of a lot of fun.

The door opened, and I turned, half expecting to see Parker standing there. Instead, it was Trudy, and she'd brought a friend. I recognized her dog's breed as a Belgian Malinois. They reminded me of a skinnier, less densely furred German Shepherd. Her's had a black and brown head, with a mostly brown body. I couldn't tell if it was a female or male.

I cast a quick glance at Smooshie because I didn't want her to scare Trudy. Pit bulls had a reputation for being aggressive. A mostly unfounded one. All dog breeds had the capacity for aggression. Pit bulls were no different in that respect. That's why it was important to be a responsible dog owner. If someone has a big dog, you have to treat every situation as if your dog might react on instinct in a way that could get them into trouble. It was the only way to keep them safe.

Keeping Smooshie safe was my number one priority. "Hold on," I said to Trudy, and I trotted over and clipped Smooshie's leash onto her harness.

Malinois are an intelligent breed with a great nose for scents. The Moonrise police force had one they used to sniff out drugs. The dog, Poirot, named for the famous Belgian detective, had been socialized from a young age, but the trainer had said they could be high strung and fiercely protective. The detective had put on a really cool demonstration where he had the dog seek out drugs hidden around a room. It had inspired me to try and play "hide the treat" with Smooshie because I was convinced she was at least as smart as Poirot.

She wasn't. It turned out she was terrible at the game.

As long as she could see it, she could retrieve it. But once, I put a biscuit under one of her blankets, and instead of tugging the blanket off her bed, she simply chewed a hole through it to retrieve her yum-yum. It was so ridiculous, I had to laugh. That's when I'd told

Parker that Smooshie would make a great drug-sniffing dog, as long as the bad guys put the drugs out in plain sight.

I stood several feet from Trudy, with Smooshie next to me, whacking me hard with her tail.

"Hold," Trudy said to her dog, and he kept still at her side. She smiled. "I swear bad weather triggers this one's bladder," she said. "Isn't that right, Magnus." She gave the dog a light scratch. Magnus was looking at us, but not in an aggressive manner. He was well-behaved like Poirot had been.

"You're not kidding," I said. "Smooshie knocked the air out of me to wake me up."

"She's such a pretty girl," Trudy said. "And she deserves an award for her bravery and heroism."

I laughed. "You mean for being a four-legged wrecking ball."

"Potatoes, puh-tah-toes." She waved her hand. "If she hadn't gotten the woven piece of the fence over, I would have been done for. Two broken legs and a possible broken back or neck. That would've started my birthday off as badly as it ended."

"I'm sorry about your party," I told her.

"Why? Did you kill that jackass?" Her question caught me off guard, but then she laughed. "I'm kidding," she said. "You were probably the only one there that didn't have a bone to pick with that man."

Okay. This conversation just got interesting. "He wasn't well-liked? Did you know him well?"

"Well enough," she said. "I've had quite the earful from Cat, you know, his wife." She shook her head. "I guess she's his widow now." Trudy licked her lips. "Lucky girl."

"Wow, you really didn't like him."

"From everything she told me, he was a controlling, manipulative, gaslighting, lying narcissist."

"Don't sugarcoat it, Trudy. Tell me how you really feel."

She chortled. "I probably shouldn't speak ill of the dead, but being dead doesn't suddenly make you a good person, no matter what someone's obituaries tell you."

I considered putting Trudy on my suspect list, but she seemed like the kind of person smart enough not to incriminate herself if she was guilty. "Do you think his wife killed him?"

Now it was Trudy's turn to be taken by surprise. "You know, I can't imagine it. She doesn't seem like the type, but who knows. If you keep someone trapped in a corner long enough, they're bound to come out fighting...or lay down and die. Cat strikes me as the laydown and die type."

I'd seen the scar on Cat's wrist. Trudy wasn't wrong about her. But people, even timid ones, could be scared into action. Just like a friendly dog. "Did you know the Maddox's before they arrived?"

Trudy shook her head. "Met Cat a week ago. They arrived the same day as Jonathan and I."

That wasn't the complete truth, but not a lie either. Once again, I couldn't help but think there was a lot of omitting happening. Cat had said Dade was an investigator for a law firm in New Mexico.

"Where are you and Jonathan from?" I asked.

"Colorado, originally," Trudy said. "But we move around. My business takes me to a lot of places."

"What business?" I asked.

She smiled. "I'm a motivational speaker," she replied. "I've been doing the talk circuit for a lot of years."

"On what topic?"

"Moving past grief and the loss of a child."

I frowned. "Greta said you only had one child."

"Well, Paul is for all intents and purposes, an only child now. But I had a daughter once."

Her voice held a deep sadness I could relate to. Daniel might not have been my biological child, but I'd raised him as best I could, and when he died, I felt like a part of me disappeared with him.

"I'm so sorry, Trudy."

She stared far off into the distance. "They say what doesn't kill you makes you stronger. I don't believe that. I think some people are already strong, so they keep surviving, and some people aren't, so they don't. It's as simple as that. But a survivor isn't made, honey." She absently rubbed Magnus's back. "That's a story we tell ourselves, so we can justify all the bad things that happen to us, those burdens we have to bear, the sacrifices we make, the losses we live with so that we can say they were for some greater purpose."

I'm feeling really motivated, I thought, *to get the hell out of here.* Trudy was a real downer. "I should get Smooshie back inside."

Trudy seemed to recall herself then. "I'm sorry, Lily. That wasn't motivational at all." She laughed. "Sometimes I can get a little melancholy, especially around my birthday. I'm not usually this fatalistic."

"It's been a fatalistic night," I told her.

She smiled. "That it has." Before I could leave, she asked, "What do you do for a living?"

At that, I smiled back. "I rescue dogs."

The grin on her face widened. "Oh, I like you. I like you a whole lot."

No lies detected. "Trudy," I said. "The feeling is mutual."

CHAPTER 11

Extremely offensive sunlight streamed into our room through our slightly parted curtain. "You've got to be kidding me."

I rolled away from the foul beam and stared at Parker. He was staring right back.

"Morning," he said.

"It sure is," I agreed. "Checking in at nighttime, you forget about pesky things like the sun melting your brain if you don't have your curtains closed all the way."

"That's my fault." He put his hand on my hip. The streaming light made his dark blue eyes sparkle like sapphires. "I must've left it open when I checked to see if the storm was still going on last night."

"Since you're stupidly handsome, I'll forgive you." I booped his nose.

He chuckled, the sound tugging at the lower parts of my body. "Did you just boop me?"

"It was that or kiss you with my dragon breath." I sniffed the air. "It's pretty bad."

"I know," he said. "I'm five inches from your face."

"Hey." I gave his shoulder a light punch. "I can criticize my bad morning breath, not you."

Parker reached out and grabbed me, yanking me to his body as he rolled on top. "I like your bad breath. It's a real turn-on." He breathed down at me. "How do you like mine?"

My eyes widened in shock, disbelief, and betrayal. "You brushed!"

He cocked his brow at me and smirked. "Did I? Or was I born naturally minty fresh?"

Parker never set off my lie detector magic. I liked to think he would never lie to me, but even when he did it in jest, it never activated my mojo. I was pretty sure it was part of our mate bond.

"Your breath was not minty fresh yesterday morning. I can attest to that." He was holding my arms over my head, but I craned my neck up, so my face was close to his. "How..." I emphasized the H sound, then added it to several of my next words, "long whhhilll you be able to stand mhhhy breath?"

Parker gave me a quick peck of a kiss, then let me go. "You win." He rolled out of bed then headed to the bathroom, closing the door between us.

Smooshie jumped up on the bed from the floor and walked up to where my head was. She licked my cheek. Her breath was about as pleasant as mine. She nudged the blanket. I held it up for her, and she crawled under then circled twice before flopping down on the mattress, her backside pressed against my outer thigh.

"I don't blame you, girl. I want to throw the covers

over my head, too." I had a headache. I wasn't sure if it was from the weather change yesterday going from the thirties in the afternoon to single digits in the middle of the night, or if it was because of the lack of sleep. I glanced over at Elvis. He was sprawled on the other bed, taking his half out of the middle. He, like Smooshie, didn't look like he planned to get up anytime soon.

"Morning, boy." His hammer of a tail hit the bed with three solid thumps.

Unfortunately, staying in bed wasn't an option for me. First thing I needed to do was tell Nadine and Reggie about my strange encounter with Trudy last night. If what the woman said was right, there were more suspects than we originally thought. So far, we'd put Cat, Billy, and Greta at the top of the list. There were even some valid reasons Marshall might make a good suspect. I got the impression the young man was infatuated with Cat, and that Dade's suspicions about the ski instructor's intentions toward his wife might've been spot on. But maybe Trudy had a place on there as well. She'd had some choice words for Dade Maddox, and none of them good. But not liking a murder victim didn't make you a killer. Something else I knew from personal experience.

"Hey," I yelled at the bathroom door. "Have you noticed that a lot of the murder victims I've stumbled over have been unsympathetic? Not all of them, of course. But it does seem like some of them, like Katherine was using her husband's private sessions with his parishioners to leverage information for power,

Donny Doyle blackmailed married women, Jock beat his wife and ruined lives, and even the guy Smooshie found in the living room wall had been a bank robber, and those weren't even the worst."

If I could have let Rowdy's killer off the hook, I would have. He had done despicable things to her, and as far as I was concerned, she should've gotten a medal for taking him out. But that was the part of me that had grown up with shifter justice. Human laws didn't work that way. It was less swift, and sometimes the wrong people were convicted, and sometimes the real criminals were let go. I'd found the process frustrating.

I heard the toilet flush. "Do you think that's a coincidence?"

"Probably," Parker said. I heard his electric razor click on. "If you look at anyone the right way, you can find their faults."

"I agree. But you have to admit, some of these guys wore their faults like blue ribbons at a state fair."

Parker came out of the bathroom with nothing but a towel around his waist. I took a second to admire his body. "What's got you on this line of thinking?"

"What?"

A slow smile crested his lips. "Am I distracting you, darling?"

"Yes." Dang, he made it hard to think when he looked that good.

He stroked his clean-shaven jawline. "Would you like me to put some clothes on?"

I shook my head. "Nope."

Parker dropped his towel on the floor. "Make your point, then join me in the shower."

"I'll make my point later." I scrambled out from under the covers, leaving Smooshie on her own, then raced past Parker to give my teeth a quick brush along with a swish of mouth wash."

"Mmm." Parker kissed me while he took off my T-shirt, and I dropped my underwear to the floor. "Fresh."

I giggled as he picked me up and carried me to the shower. He turned on the water, and the rush of cold stole my breath.

I let out a noise that sent Smooshie scrambling from the covers and barreling into the bathroom.

"What fresh hell is this?" I asked, grabbing a terrycloth robe from a hook on the bathroom wall.

Parker stood outside the shower and held his hand under the spray. After a few moments, he shook his head. "It's not getting any warmer."

I went over to the landline phone in our room and picked it up. I pressed 9 for the concierge.

"Guest services, Ada speaking. How can I assist you?" a woman answered.

"This is room eighteen. There's no hot water."

"We're aware of the situation," she said. "Unfortunately, the power is still out to the mountain, and the generators don't power the hot water heaters. We apologize for the inconvenience, and we hope to have the service restored as soon as possible. Would you like a call to your room when the situation is resolved?"

"No, thanks," I told her. I wasn't planning to stay in the room all day.

"Is there anything else I can help you with?"

"Are you guys serving breakfast this morning?"

"We have a full buffet in the restaurant until ten a.m.," she said. "Free of charge."

I wonder if the food storage was also not on the generator. Whatever the reason, I was starving, and I wasn't about to turn down free food. "Thank you, Ada, for your help."

"My pleasure. Anything else?"

"Nope, I'm good." I hung up the phone and frowned at Parker. "Still no outside power and no hot water."

Parker's lips thinned with annoyance. "You know, I thought it was weird when we ran out of hot water last night. I didn't think that happened in hotels."

"There's good news, though. Apparently, they are feeding everyone, on the house, in the restaurant." I didn't want to be stuck with eggs and oatmeal, but if I was being honest, right now, I'd eat shoe leather if it was the only thing on the menu. "We should get dressed and get down there before all the good bits disappear."

Parker laughed and shook his head. "Let's get you fed before you shrivel up and blow away."

"Dang, Lily," Nadine complained. "Did you leave any bacon for the rest of us?"

The dining room was filled with the aroma of savory smoked meats, along with the sweet and spicy scents of cinnamon, apple, and maple syrup. Thirty or so guests, either sitting down at a table or shuffling along the buffet line, filled the restaurant. There were many who I didn't recognize, but several had been guests at the party the night before. And of course, there was my family. Parker, Buzz, Greer, and Reggie were currently in line for food. Nadine had sent Buzz to get his plate first. He'd tried to get her to go before him, but she'd insisted.

"There's still some left up there," I told Nadine as I sat down at the table where she'd been sitting with the triplets. I took Jericho from the stroller and put him on my knee. Like his siblings, he had several teeth and had been on solid food since four months old. "Besides, I'm going to share with my buddy here."

Jericho had red hair and green eyes like Buzz and me. Jackson and Journey looked more like Nadine, and they were smaller than Jericho as well. All three of them were supposed to be human, not shifters, but sometimes I wondered if Jericho didn't have a little werecougar in him.

He let out a joyous squeal of delight as I wagged a piece of bacon in front of him. Even if he wasn't a shifter, he still took after his favorite Aunt Lily. The boy was a bottomless pit.

"The waitress said they were going to bring three highchairs out for us," Nadine said. "I don't want to be cleaning out this stroller if they have to eat in it. I love my children, but dear Lord, they're messy."

"You go ahead and get your food," I told Nadine. "I'll watch the babies."

"Bay-bay-bay-bay," Jericho babbled as he gnawed on the small piece of bacon I gave him. I broke off two more pieces and handed them to Jackson and Journey. "If I had enough lap, all three of you would be here," I told them.

My energy was low after yesterday, so I'd nabbed eight pieces of bacon, a couple of scoops of eggs, some sausage links that looked a little gray but smelled okay, a bowl of cheesy grits, sausage gravy, and a couple of buttermilk biscuits. I hoped it was enough to fill me up.

Trudy waved at me from three tables away. Her husband, son, and his wife were all sitting with her. I nodded and waved back. I didn't see Cat Maddox anywhere. If she didn't come down for breakfast, I'd check on her. I could understand why Marshall felt so protective of Cat. I barely knew the woman, and I had the impulse to make sure she was safe. Even if it was from herself.

I took a bite of grits. They were creamy and as cheesy as I'd hoped for. Parker sat down next to me, and he pulled the stroller to him, then retrieved both Journey and Jackson and put them on his knees. He bounced them back and forth, much to their giggling delight. Journey was fearless. She loved high octane play. Buzz had taken to throwing her up in the air, and she loved every minute of flying. She was going to be a daredevil. Jackson, on the other hand, was the most subdued of the bunch. He liked to play with blocks, do puzzles, and that sort of activity. I know it didn't mean he would turn into Einstein, but I was glad that each of them had their own things that made them unique.

Billy Brandish walked into the dining room and held

up his hand. "If I can get your attention for one second, folks," he started. "I have some updates."

The murmuring guests immediately grew silent.

"The electric company isn't sure when they'll be able to get the transformer fixed," he said.

There was a collective groan at this news.

Billy tried to mollify us. "I know it's not what you wanted to hear, and I apologize for the inconvenience, but Mother Nature is wreaking havoc on us right now. Thanks to the blizzard, there are power outages in more places than in our little part of the mountain. We are just going to have to wait until they can get to us."

"What about the hot water?" someone asked. And no, I wasn't that someone, but I was curious as well.

"I'm working with maintenance on a solution for the hot water heaters. They use up a lot of power that we need elsewhere in the lodge, like the furnace and the lights. But if the electricity doesn't come back on by tomorrow, we'll figure out a way to get those tanks heated."

"Can we leave?" Trudy's son Paul asked.

I knew the answer would be a big no. At least not until Paul was cleared as a suspect in Dade's murder.

"Sorry," Billy said. "The roads are still closed. The highway department is working as quickly as they can, but there are a lot of roads and only a few plows. They tell me they can have the roads cleared by tomorrow."

Nadine was heading to the front of the room to join Billy. She leaned in and said something to him. She kept her voice quiet, but I heard her say, "We talked about this already. I'm in charge of this murder inquiry, and no one is leaving until we get some answers."

Billy's brow creased as his lips stretched into a grim line. He gave her a curt nod. "I'm going to ask that guests please make yourselves available to Officer Nadine Booth for a few questions this afternoon," he said.

"Deputy Sheriff Booth," Nadine corrected.

"Deputy Sheriff," Billy amended.

"If I haven't already talked to you, assume that I will need to," Nadine told the dining room. "It's not a big deal. I just have a few questions, is all."

"So, it's true," a man said. "Someone was killed here last night."

"Are we safe?" a woman asked.

"This is insane," another woman said. "You can't keep us locked up with a murderer all weekend."

Billy rolled his eyes and groaned. "This is exactly what I wanted to avoid," he hissed.

"Hey," Nadine snapped at the guests. "If you try to leave this resort and get stuck outside in zero-degree weather because you go off the road and there's no one available to rescue you, then you won't have to worry about a murderer killing you, now will you?" She clapped her hands to command their silence. "The roads are impassable, that is a fact. Besides, we don't really know what happened at this point. That's why I need to talk to everyone, whether at dinner, in the lobby, or in your rooms. You might have seen something important, and you just don't know it yet."

Billy sighed, clearly frustrated. "That's all the

updates," he said. "I will let you know more when I know more."

Greta Michaels excused herself from the table and followed the irritated resort manager as he left the room.

I took another bite of my grits as I watched her go.

Nadine came back to the table. "I hope I didn't come off as harsh, but these people are trying my last nerve."

"I think you were the exact right amount of harsh," I told her. "They needed real talk." I wagged my spoon at the door. "Speaking of real talk. I'd love to sit in when you speak to Greta. She just took off after Billy."

Nadine nodded. "Consider it done." She arched her brow. "Much like those grits, the plot thickens."

"Oh, no." I grimaced. "That's so bad."

She cracked a smile. "I hate myself a little for it."

I shook my head and smirked, "As you should."

The corny analogy aside, Nadine wasn't wrong. Greta didn't know that we knew about the photos. Did Greta even know about the photos? Why would she risk going after her lover with her husband sitting right next to her unless she was desperate? And did desperation make her a killer?

CHAPTER 12

The lingering scent of primer and fresh paint nauseated me. Or it could've been the revenge of the gray sausage and buffet scrambled eggs. Whatever the reason, I was giving myself fifty-fifty odds that I'd make it through the interviews with Nadine before losing my breakfast.

Greta sat across from us at an eight-foot event table. Nadine made a show of checking over her notes as she casually moved the bubble mailer with the incriminating photographs from one side of her clipboard to the other.

"Can we get on with this?" Greta asked. "I have a massage at eleven."

Nadine peered up at her then back down at her notes.

"What? I'm stressed out," Greta complained. "A massage is the only way to get my chakras back in alignment. My fifth and tenth are all out of sorts. Reversed, I think. I mean, they feel like they're reversed."

"There are only seven chakras," my badass cop bestie said with a great deal of authority. "And number five, located," she pressed two fingers behind the back of her neck at the base, "right about here, is your center for communication and honesty. So are you telling me your honesty chakra needs a good scrubbing?"

I wasn't sure how Nadine knew all that, but I let out a quiet, "yesss," and resisted the urge to snap in Greta's face.

"I don't know what you're getting at," she sputtered. "Are you accusing me of something? Do I need a lawyer?"

I made a face as her incensed-induced spittle dotted the surface of the table. Yuck.

"I'm not accusing you of anything," Nadine responded. "Yet. And if you can satisfy a few questions of mine, I'll happily let you get to your massage so you can get an attitude adjustment."

"Pah." Greta rolled her eyes. "Fine. Ask your questions already."

It was interesting to note that while Greta was undoubtedly annoyed and frightened, she paid hardly any attention to the envelope. Nadine kept moving around the bait, but the woman wasn't interested in getting on the hook.

Nadine tapped her pen against the clipboard. "Did you see the deceased, Dade Maddox, at any time during the twenty-four hours leading up to the party last night?"

Greta chewed the side of her cheek. Her pink lipstick oozed into the creases at the corners of her mouth as she moved her pursed lips side to side. After several long, dramatic minutes, she shook her head. "Not that I can recall."

Ding, ding, ding. Greta was a liar, liar.

Nadine pivoted her gaze to me. I shook my head. She turned her attention back to Greta then pounded her palm against the table. "That's one lie," she told the woman. "Now, you owe me two truths."

Greta leaned back, her eyes wide with surprise and indignation. "Well, I—"

"—better answer my question," Nadine said, cutting her protest off. "When did you see Dade Maddox? And don't leave any encounters out." Nadine glared at Greta. "I will know if you do."

The woman let out an exasperated sigh then threw up her hands. "Fine. I saw him a little while before the party. Maybe an hour before."

"Doing what?" I asked, then glanced sharply to Nadine. I wasn't trying to take over her interview.

Greta glared at me. "Are you a police officer, too?"

"Ms. Mason is a consultant," Nadine explained. She nodded at me, then said, "So answer her question. What was he doing?"

"He was with...." She let out a noise of frustration. "He was talking to my husband."

"Why was he talking to Paul?" I gave Nadine another apologetic look.

"Go ahead, Lily." She knew about my powers to persuade the truth out of people. "I don't mind. If you don't hit all the questions I want to know, I'll jump in."

I loved that Nadine cared more about getting to the

truth than she did about ego. "Thanks," I told her. I focused my attention back on Greta. "What was Dade doing with Paul?"

"I don't know," Greta said, and it rang true.

"But?"

"But...they were arguing. And before you ask, I don't know what about. As I said, I don't know why my husband was talking to the loathsome man."

Nadine leaned forward and rested her elbows on the table. "So, you knew Dade from sometime before."

"Is that a question?" Greta's tone dripped with sarcasm.

"It's one you better get to answering," Nadine said. She pointed to a wall clock. "Or you're going to be late for a lot more than just your massage."

Greta's expression grew strangled. "Oh, fine," she breathed out. "I heard some indelicate things about him, but I didn't actually know him."

"Who gave you this information about the victim?"

Greta snorted her disbelief. "That man was no victim."

"Technically, getting murdered makes him exactly that," I said to her. "You're not doing yourself any favors by not getting honest with us."

She rolled her eyes. "Is this supposed to be one of those *the truth will set you free* moments?"

Nadine rapped her knuckles on the table in front of Greta. "That's exactly what kind of moment this is."

"I won't betray my family," Greta said.

Man, this was a secret she meant to keep. Nadine raised a questioning brow at me, and I shrugged.

"Fine," Nadine said. "You're so worried about betrayal. What do you have to say about these?" She slid the bubble mailer over to Greta.

Greta dropped her hands below the table as if she were being asked to touch a live snake. "What's this?"

"Have a look inside," Nadine said.

"I don't want to," Greta shot back.

"For heaven's sake." Nadine grabbed the unopened end of the envelope and dumped its contents onto the table. The pictures came out upside down. She let go of the mailer then turned the photos over.

Greta gasped. Then she did something that neither Nadine nor I could've seen coming. She grabbed the pictures, crumpled them up, and shoved them in her mouth.

I was stunned into inaction.

Nadine, luckily, got over her shock quicker than me. She lunged across the table and grabbed Greta's arms. "Get the photos out of her mouth," she yelled at me. "Don't let her swallow them."

I ran around the table. Greta was a taller woman than me, so when she stood up, I kicked the back of her knee to put her back in the chair. I placed her in a headlock with my left arm then started digging the saliva-covered pictures from between her teeth. When she tried to bite me, I tightened the bend between my forearm and my bicep then dug my elbow into her sternum. She opened her mouth to scream her pain, and I hooked the wad with my finger and flicked it onto the floor.

"Noooo," Greta cried. "Where did you get those? How?"

I let go of her neck, picked up the wet, mangled photos and tossed them on the table. My fingers were coated in Greta's spit. Ew. Where was a sanitizing wet wipe when you needed one?

Greta slumped forward and sobbed. "My, God, Paul. He doesn't know. Tell me he doesn't know."

This was becoming a lot more dramatic than necessary. "Why cheat?" I asked her.

"I...I'm lonely," she said. "Billy made me feel...." She sniffed. "He made me feel like I wasn't by myself anymore. Paul is so wrapped up with his mother's foundation. Don't get me wrong, it's why I fell in love with him. But he gets so hyper-focused on work to the point that it can feel like I don't exist." She clasped her hands together. "Please, please don't tell him."

"Then tell me who told you about Dade Maddox," Nadine said flatly. "If you do that, I'll try to keep your affair out of the report."

She didn't make any promises. If it turned out to be pertinent to the crime, the affair would come out. Frankly, I thought it was going to come out one way or another anyhow, but who was I to piss on the parade.

Greta wiped her eyes with the back of her hand, causing mascara to flake on her red cheeks. "Trudy," she said. "I overheard Trudy talking to Paul about Maddox."

"What did she say about him?"

"If I tell you, I'll lose Paul." Tears crested her eyes again. "He is devoted to his mother. He'll never forgive me."

Nadine pinned Greta with her gaze. "Tell me."

"Trudy said that Maddox is the reason Piper Downs got away with killing her daughter." Her expression was filled with anguish. "She said she was going to make him pay."

"Let me get this straight," Nadine said. "Are you telling me you heard your mother-in-law plotting to kill Dade Maddox?"

Greta hiccupped, then nodded. "You can't tell her that I told you," she pleaded. "But, yes, that's exactly what I'm telling you."

Nadine looked at me. "I think my suspect list got a lot shorter."

CHAPTER 13

I went to the bathroom and scrubbed my hands for a full two minutes, then I threw up and scrubbed my hands again before rejoining Nadine in the makeshift interrogation room.

"Next time, you get to pull crap out of the witness's mouth," I told her.

She shook her head, disbelief plain on her face. "I'll admit, I didn't see that one coming." She scowled. "I didn't make copies of the photos. If they have to be used at the trial, it's going to be really embarrassing on the stand when I have to explain the missing pieces and the teeth marks."

I snickered. "I'll be in the front row for that. Man, oh, man. If that happens, you will never hear the end of it from Opal and Pearl." The two elderly sisters liked to go watch trials when they could, the same way some people liked to go to movies. It was their chosen form of entertainment.

"Wipe that smile off your face, Lily. You're supposed to be on my side," Nadine whined.

"I'm one-hundred-percent on your side," I said on a stifled chuckle.

"You're the worst," she said. "I guess we should talk to Trudy Waddle next. What do you think, Lily? Do you believe she could've orchestrated this murder?"

"Do I think she could? Yes, she's smart and calculating. I'm not sure that means she did it, though." I tapped my lower lip. "At least, not alone. After all, she'd just entered the room when the lights went out. And that's the part that keeps throwing me off. There were a few tables behind us. Marshall had taken the spill onto the floor. Trudy came in like a *grande dame*, making an entrance. The lights went out. There's no way she could have made it all the way past me, stabbed Dade, then got back to her position near the door. According to Reggie, he hit his head, whether an accident or someone else hit him, at least twelve hours before the party. Then someone figured out how to administer a certainly lethal dose of some drug, only then to stab him." I shook my head. "How does any of this make sense."

"What about her husband, Jonathan? Could he have snuck into the back of the suite at some point in time and...."

"And wait for a semi-truck to slide off the road and take out a transformer?" I shook my head. "I don't buy it. Besides, a butter knife is the last weapon you'd pick if you planned to kill someone, right?"

"Crime of opportunity, then," Nadine concluded,

then shook her head. "Only the first two parts of this murder tell a different story of premeditation."

"Maybe it's both. As we've heard several times, he wasn't a nice man. Maybe more than one person or persons wanted him dead."

Nadine sat down and propped her feet up on the table. "You know this sounds crazy. There's enough mud on this case to hang a jury."

GETTING TRUDY IN FOR A STATEMENT PROVED harder than it should've been. The snow had stopped at six in the morning, and while the power hadn't been restored, she and her husband had decided to go skiing.

"I can't believe they are chancing the slopes after what happened yesterday," Reggie said. "And Christ, the snow might've stopped, but it is still bitterly cold out here."

Nadine jumped up and down in place to generate heat. "You're not kidding."

Both my friends and I were wearing puffy winters coats, insulated pants, mittens, and boots, along with thermal ski masks that covered most of our faces. If it hadn't been for the fact that our outfits were yellow, lavender, and cornflower blue—mine was the lavender one—we would've looked like polar bank robbers.

I'll admit, all geared up, I wasn't feeling the cold the way they were. "Come on. I see Trudy. She's wearing a pink and yellow ensemble at the top of the hill."

"Where's the husband?" Nadine asked.

Marshall, who was on the bunny slope, walked over to us. "Can I give you ladies a lesson?"

"We're not here for the skiing," Reggie said. Then she gave him a disapproving look. "Where's your sling?"

Marshall took off his thick glove and flexed his fingers on his splinted wrist side. "It's feeling much better today, Doctor Crawford," he said in an *aww, shucks* way. "You have the magic touch."

Reggie rolled her eyes, but I could see the slight slip of a smile. "Whatever," she told him. "Just make sure you get an x-ray. The resort should pay for it."

"As if," Marshall said.

"It's covered under work comp," Reggie told him. "Make sure you fill out an accident report with your boss, and when you go to the hospital, tell them it was a work injury. That will get the ball rolling."

Marshall put his glove back on. "Thanks, Doc. Sweet tip."

"Yeah, Doc. Sweet tip," I teased. She ignored me.

"There." Nadine pointed at the slope as a man wearing gray and blue outerwear zipped down the hill like he'd been born with skis on his feet.

"Damn, he's good," Reggie said.

"He should be," Marshall said. "He was the downhill silver medalist at the nineteen eighty-eight winter Olympics."

"Wowza," Nadine said with clear admiration. "I wasn't even born in eighty-eight."

Reggie scoffed. "I feel old."

"You're not *that* old," Nadine said.

I giggled. "Stop helping," I told her. "Reggie, you are still a hot babe. Besides, age is just a number, right?"

"Neither of you is making me feel better. Let's just move on past this. I'm perfectly delighted being in my forties."

"No way, Doc," Marshall said. "Lily's right. You're a total snack."

"Uhm, thanks, I guess." Even with the ski mask on, I could tell she was both flattered and embarrassed by the compliment.

"Uh-oh." I pointed in Trudy's direction. "Unless we want to wait an hour for her to climb the mountain, we better grab her."

"We have a guy ferrying skiers up and down on the snowmobile," Marshall said.

"The one you wrecked?"

He shook his head. "That one's toast."

"Still, we don't want to be out here any more than we have to be," Nadine jumped in. "Marshall, you've got skis. Will you glide on over there and tell Mrs. Waddle I need to talk to her?"

Marshall gave Nadine an adorable salute and said, "Sure thing, Deputy." The young man stepped into his skis with ease then rapidly made his way over to Trudy.

They were far enough away, not even my supernatural hearing could overhear their conversation. But I could see Marshall talking with his hands then pointing in our direction. Trudy leaned around him. She smiled. Waved. Pulled her glasses down then used her ski poles to push herself onto the slope. Seconds later, she was racing down the mountain.

I blinked at the blur of pink, yellow, and white powdery snow. "This is the photograph incident all over again. At least she's not trying to eat the mountain."

Nadine slapped her hand against her jacket. "Why is this happening?"

Reggie whistled. "She's really good too."

"Is she trying to escape?" Nadine asked. "Surely she's not ignorant enough to think she can get away."

I could no longer see her or Jonathan. "She looks like she's doing a pretty good job of getting away if you ask me."

"I am not asking you," Nadine quipped.

"Oh, here comes Marshall."

Marshall skied back to us. His expression was forlorn. "She said to tell you that she's on vacation."

Nadine shook a mitted fist into the air and declared, "So are we, damn it."

It turned out that Trudy—while making our lives a little more difficult—wasn't actually trying to escape the mountain. She and Jonathan hitched a ride with the guy driving the snowmobile back to the top of the slope, where she had the driver deposit her next to us.

"You could've skipped the theatrics," Nadine told her.

"And what fun would that have been?" Trudy asked. "Well, I suppose if you insist on interviewing me, Deputy, we better get to it?"

"I'd like to take this to a warmer location," Reggie said.

"Like the Caribbean," Nadine agreed. "Whose idea was it to vacation in the frozen tundra?"

I gave her a bland look because she knew darn well, I'd been the one to suggest the trip. In my defense, Parker and I were on a budget, and there were only so many affordable winter resorts that were within driving distance of Moonrise. So, I gave her the bird.

Nadine snickered. "Come on, Mrs. Waddle. We'll all be more comfortable inside."

"I'm afraid if you believe that, then you don't know me, dear," Trudy said. "But I'm nothing if not cooperative."

I tried, unsuccessfully, not to laugh as we escorted Trudy back to the lodge.

CHAPTER 14

Trudy had changed into butter-soft, pale blue leggings and an oversized, mocha cashmere sweater, finished with a pair of cute fuzzy brown boots. She sat down at the event table and crossed her legs as she studied Nadine, Reggie, and me.

"You three are barking up the wrong tree if you believe that I had anything to do with that man's death," she finally said. "I was nowhere near him when he was killed."

"When was the last time you saw him before the party?" Nadine asked.

"You mean the party that never happened, thanks to Dade inconveniently getting murdered?" Her tone was blasé and indifferent.

"Answer the question," Nadine prodded.

"All right." She glanced away for a moment, then said, "He stopped by my hotel room early yesterday morning to grab Jonathan for a workout."

"You didn't see him after that?"

Trudy shrugged and shook her head. "Nope. Not until the party. And then, only briefly." A smile tugged at her lips.

"You really do hate the guy, don't you?" I asked.

"Not anymore," Trudy assured me. "He's gone. Nothing left of him to hate."

"What did he do to you?" My emotions were on edge, and I felt the push of my mojo a little harder than I'd intended.

"He made a mockery out of my daughter's life, and for that, he can die a thousand deaths." She blinked, surprised that the words had come out of her own mouth.

"Who's Piper Downs?" Nadine asked her.

Trudy looked even more startled. "Where did you hear that name?"

"Is Piper Downs at the resort?"

The woman stared hard at Nadine for a moment, then laughed. "You have absolutely nothing, do you? You are just grasping at straws, hoping one of them will be strong enough to keep a hold of. I like you, Lily." She shifted her gaze to me. "So, I'm going to throw you a bone. Piper Downs is a pharmaceutical research company, not a person. Ten years ago, my daughter Olivia, a lovely girl who was only nineteen years old, signed up for one of their drug trials. You see, she'd had depression on and off since puberty. Piper Downs was experimenting with antianxiety medications. Four months into the drug trials, Liv killed herself." Pain flashed across Trudy's face as she recalled the story.

"Now, I might have believed, foolishly, that Liv's

death was a senseless tragedy that couldn't have been prevented, except one of the researchers in the study became a whistleblower. It turned out that twenty percent of the subjects in the study, especially ones with a history of depression, had suicidal thoughts while on the new drug. And fifteen percent attempted suicide, and five percent, the percentage category Liv fell in, ended in death."

"Did Maddox work for Piper Downs?" Nadine asked, trying to understand where this was all leading.

"No," she said. "He worked for the law firm that represented Piper Downs in our class-action lawsuit against the assault and negligent homicide. That man dug around in my daughter's life and found a Pinstabook post from when she was sixteen where she commented about how everyone would be better off without her." Trudy balled her hands into fists. "She was sixteen. She'd just been dumped by her first boyfriend. But that man twisted what he found, then paid off some of her so-called friends to lie and say she talked about killing herself multiple times."

Trudy's eyes glittered with fresh tears. Even though our situations weren't the same, her story brought up a fresh wash of grief and guilt through me for my brother Daniel. It had been dark, experimental magic that had killed him, not bad, experimental drugs, but like with her Liv, Danny had been murdered by a powerful group who only cared about their end goals. The death toll they left behind them was a means to an end, but Danny and Liv hadn't been expendable to the people who loved them.

Danny had been more than collateral damage. He had been mine.

I squeezed my eyes closed for a moment, fighting to control the feelings this case had stirred up in me. I felt Reggie's hand on mine. I glanced at her. "You okay?" she mouthed.

I nodded. A half-truth. I wasn't okay, but I would be.

"What happened then?" Nadine asked Trudy as if we all didn't already know the answer.

"If what he did to Liv wasn't bad enough, he managed to find or manufacture equally damning dirt on all the other claimants as well. The judge granted Piper Downs a complete dismissal of all charges." She leaned forward. "With prejudice."

"That's horrible," Reggie said. "If it had been my daughter, I'd have wanted to kill him, too."

Trudy heaved a sigh. "You don't get it. I didn't want to kill him. I wanted to turn and burn him. I wanted dirt that I knew he had on Piper Downs, and then I wanted to bury him, his law firm, and that pharmaceutical company with it."

"What makes you think he had dirt on the company?"

"Because he is the kind of man who likes to have leverage. It's his currency." She leaned back and relaxed her hands. "Do you know that his wife was one of the plaintiffs? I followed their romance on social media. Cat doesn't have a lot of filter, so she posts everything going on in her life. I couldn't believe it when Maddox started dating her. The nerve of the man. He'd buried her future under his rot and greed, and then he made her a possession."

"Does she know?" I asked. "That her husband was the one who tanked the lawsuit?"

Trudy shrugged. "It's hard to say. From what she told me, Cat has suffered some setbacks over the ten years since her encounter with Piper Downs, including three suicide attempts. But she told me that the past year has been one of the best of her life, at least where her depression was concerned."

This story painted Dade Maddox as someone who didn't care about anyone but himself... except his wife. I wondered if his employers knew about his leverage. Did he have goods on them?

"Did Dade Maddox know you were Olivia's mother?" Nadine asked gently.

Trudy bowed her head then looked up at us with a slow blink. "A lot can change in a decade. During the trial, I was a frumpy, middle-aged mom named Gertrude Michaels. A year later, I had lost fifty pounds, got in shape, dyed my hair blond, and married a man who called me Trudy, and that's who I became. I thought I had a handle on my grief. Hell, I've been coaching people on love and loss for over five years now. But when I saw Cat's Pinstabook story about how she and Dade were going to be vacationing in Waggin' Trails for a couple of weeks, it stirred up a lot of anger."

"What did you think would happen?"

"I don't know," she said. "Not this, though."

Trudy's story about Dade Maddox was horrific, sad,

and enraging, but none of it answered the one question that needed to be answered.

"Trudy," I said. "Did you kill Dade?"

She hesitated for a moment, then shook her head in denial. "No," she confessed. "But I wish I had."

That statement was one hundred percent true.

"Does this put us back at square one?" Reggie asked after Nadine let Trudy go. "I really thought we had a good suspect with that one."

"We still do," Nadine said. "We know Lily's mojo works, but it won't be convincing evidence for the local cops. She has means and motive. And if her whole family is involved, they could've created the opportunities."

"But she didn't do it." I got up from the table. My stomach roiled as bile bit at the back of my throat. "I need some food and fresh air."

Nadine walked over and put her arm around my shoulder. "Are you okay?"

"You know how they say the past comes back to haunt you? Well, mine has been saying *Boo!* for two days. I'm having a lot of feelings that I thought I'd gotten over."

"Is this about your brother?"

I nodded. I'd told Nadine and Reggie the vanilla version of how Danny had died, so they knew that I'd moved to Moonrise after his murderers had paid for their crimes. Knowing that his killers were all dead had brought me a surprising amount of peace. So, why was my psyche reopening old wounds now? Ugh. I was finally happy. Happier than I'd ever been in my entire life. Maybe that was the reason.

I'd stopped waiting for the other shoe to drop, and this case was life's way of saying it was still holding the boot.

Reggie put her arms around both Nadine and me. The three of us melted into a group hug. "You know what will make Lily feel better?" Reggie asked. "Lunch."

"Lunch sounds really good," I said. "But no more gray sausage."

Nadine snerked. "I could've told you that was a bad idea."

"Then you should've."

"You were already eating by the time I got back to the table, then the whole announcement thing went down...." Nadine pressed her temple to the top of my head. "We're here for you, Lily. We're family, and whatever makes you happy makes us happy, and whatever hurts you—"

"We'll hunt it down and kill it so it can never hurt you again," Reggie said with a ferocity that shocked us all.

Nadine and I locked eyes for a moment, then looked at Reggie, then we all started laughing.

"I love you guys," I told them. "I don't say it nearly enough, but I do."

"You show us every day, Lils," Nadine replied. "Every damn day."

"And we love you right back, sister."

I'd lost my brother, but life had given me two sisters,

an uncle, a father, and a mate. "Thanks, guys. I didn't know how much I needed this."

A sharp knock at the door broke up the *Lily-pity-party*. The door opened, and Parker poked his head in. "You guys ready to eat?"

"And then some." I crossed the room to him and slid my arms around his waist. "How are the kids?"

"Smooshie has wanted to go in and out a dozen times. Elvis officially hates the cold weather and Smooshie. Mostly because she loves it. How are the interviews going?"

"No killers yet." I gave his chin a peck. "I'm sorry I'm ignoring you for this."

"It's what you do, Lils. You have a gift for solving crimes. And while it's not my thing, I'm a-okay with it being yours. So no worries. I'm happy to hold down the furry-four-legged fort.

"I don't deserve you," I told him. "What's on the lunch menu?"

He wiggled his brows at me, then winked. "The power's still out, so no dessert."

Nadine, who'd finished packing up her notes, blurted out, "What do you mean, no dessert? That's a bunch of bull. Mamma needs her sugary carbs."

I laughed and gave Parker's earlobe a light nip. In a low voice, I growled, "Yeah, mamma needs her sugary carbs."

Reggie giggled.

Nadine rolled her eyes. "Don't ruin dessert for me. With three toddlers running my life, dessert is the only thing that keeps me going."

"I agree, wholeheartedly," Parker said. "Dessert gets me going too."

"I can't hear this." Nadine put her hands over her ears as we exited the room. "I'm not listening to you."

CHAPTER 15

There was no lunch buffet.

I knew buffets were kind of gross, and the one from the morning had surely given me food poisoning, but still, there was something to be said for "all you can eat." Before moving to Moonrise, I'd never eaten at one. A restaurant like that in a shifter town wouldn't stay in business long. But, when Parker took me to the Golden Steakhouse for the first time, I was in werecougar heaven. I'd finished off a pan of fried chicken by myself, and other than a few judgmental looks from other patrons and staff, no one said a single word about it.

"Why are you looking so grumpy, Lily?" Greer asked as I perused the menu.

"No reason," I lied. The fact that we had to order from a menu meant waiting up to half an hour or more for food, as well. There was no waiting in a buffet! "Just trying to decide what to order." The prices on these lunch specials weren't cheap, ranging anywhere from fifteen to twenty-five dollars. "I don't suppose lunch is on the house like breakfast was?"

"Nope, darling," Parker said. "No such luck. But you get what you want. We're fine."

I knew what our finances were since I paid most of the bills. Parker wasn't wrong. We were doing okay financially. We weren't in debt, our utilities were paid early every month, and we had a few thousand between the checking and the savings. It was the most stable I'd ever been, but I'd lived hand to mouth, paycheck to paycheck, and dealt with the bank owning my home for too many years before Moonrise. The home my parents had provided for me. I never wanted to feel that vulnerable again. So, I penny-pinched.

"I'm just going to get the open face meatloaf sandwich with extra mash potatoes and gravy." I scoped out the sides. "I think I want the fried okra, too."

"Then you shall have all of that," Parker said. He slid his hand over my thigh, and I interlocked my fingers with his. "Whatever you want."

"A hot shower would be a good start," I grumbled before realizing I'd said it out loud. I gave Parker a contrite look. "I'm sorry." I extended my apology to the rest of the table. "I think the lack of sleep and creature comforts is making me edgy." I set the menu down as the call of nature, in the form of a full bladder, beckoned. "Order for me, will you?" I asked Parker. "I need to find the bathroom."

"Sure." He got up and pulled my chair out for me. "You want a Coke to go with it?"

I gave him a quick kiss. "Yep, and ask for extra

catsup."

"You got it."

I wasn't in the lobby bathroom long. After I washed my hands, I exited the door and ran smack into the resort manager.

"Ope, sorry," he said as he jumped sideways to avoid a collision with me.

"For what?" I asked. "I'm the one who barreled out the door."

He gave me a *yeesh* face, then said, "Still...." He left it hanging there.

I got it. People in Missouri apologized for everything, even if they weren't at fault. I couldn't walk through a crowded bar without every person I bumped into saying, "Ope, sorry." It was nice, though. No one in Paradise Falls apologized for anything. Even when they were in the wrong.

"Have you been updated about the power or when the roads will be cleared?"

Billy exhaled noisily. "I've been on the phone with both the electric company and the D. O. T. several times today. Believe me when I say I want the power back and the roads cleared as badly as all of you. I have a corpse in my motel, and we are trapped with whoever did it until the mountain opens back up."

"I'm sure it's stressful," I told him. The image of Greta and him in the photos made me wonder if he was stressed about something more than roads and power. Maybe Billy was someone who needed a closer watch. Impulsively, I asked, "Did you know that Maddox was watching you?"

Billy snapped to attention and cleared his throat. "I don't have any idea what you're talking about."

"Lie," I said. "Try again."

"Why would anyone watch me? It's preposterous."

"Lie." I twirled my finger. "Third times a charm. Tell me why Maddox was taking pictures of you and a certain married woman."

Billy held up his hands as a few guests passed by us. "Keep your voice down," he whispered harshly. His palms and his fingers were long and slender, reminding me of a stick figure drawing. "I have my reputation to maintain, not to mention the lady's reputation."

"Then tell me the truth, and I will stop pressing you in public about it."

"Not here," he gritted out.

"I won't be going anywhere alone with you, Billy."

His expression grew incredulous. "You can't possibly think...."

"I can, but you're only one possibility until you're not. Help me put you in the *not a killer* column, Billy."

"If you must know," he seethed. "Then follow me." He walked to a secluded area in the lobby where we could be seen but not heard. When he was sure we were out of earshot of guests and staff, he said, "Waggin' Trails is having a lot of...uhm, financial trouble. There's a large company that is trying to buy the lodge and all the property surrounding it. They want to turn it into a high-end ski resort that caters to wealthy clients."

I'd noticed the lodge was less than pristine since our arrival. Everything was a bit on the shabby side. Still, I'd assumed that a place that catered to people with pets, there had to be a certain amount of wear and tear expected. "What about the dogs?"

"No dogs," he said. "They are going to make it a no pets allowed experience."

Well, that sucked. The reason I picked this place was that it was hard to find vacations that not only allowed pets but also weren't located in areas with breed-specific bans—that breed being pit bull, of course. "And what did Maddox photographing you have to do with the pending sale of this place?"

"That's just it," Billy said. "The owners don't want to sell. Maddox blackmailed me with the pictures to get me to go along with his scheme."

Again, with the partial truths. Gah! "Can't anyone around here just be honest? Are you in love with Greta?"

"No," he admitted. "But I am very fond of her."

"Well, bully for you." I stifled the urge to throat punch him. "So, tell me what happened when he tried to blackmail you."

"I told him he could go to Hell. This resort is my home and, contrary to appearances, I like my job."

"What was Maddox's counteroffer?"

Billy shuffled his feet, obviously uncomfortable. "He told me that if I helped him, he would make sure that I stayed on as resort manager with a large bump in pay."

"Since blackmail hadn't worked, he'd resorted to bribery. Is that the picture you're painting here?"

Billy sighed, then nodded. "Pretty much." He held out his hands palm up. "All I had to do was make sure a few things were broken and not up to code. A safety inspector is going to arrive on Monday to make sure the owners would be forced to sell or pay a lot of fines they can't afford."

"Diabolical," I said. A notion popped into my head. "The ski lift. Was that you?"

Billy blanched. His hands began to shake. "I didn't know the Waddles were going to use it. I had closed down the slope."

I gave him the stink eye. "That's not exactly true, is it? I heard Marshall say that Dade Maddox had rented it out privately for that hour. That's the reason the slope was shut down." I narrowed my gaze on him. "You meant for Dade to be on the lift when it jerked to a stop."

"I...I...I did no such thing," he blustered.

I arched a brow at him.

"I wasn't trying to kill him," he amended.

That was also a partial truth. I suspected Billy hadn't thought his plan through very well before putting it into action. "It's not a leap to go from attempted murder to actual murder," I told him.

I pressed him harder. "Why would you try to take out Dade if he made you such a sweet deal?"

Billy turned on his heel and walked across the lobby to a door near the check-in counter. If I wanted answers, and I did, then I had no choice but to follow. He waved at the two women, who both looked bored, then opened the door. He whistled, and a brown and white corgi came running down the narrow hall. It jumped into Billy's arms, and he swung the cute baby in a half-circle.

"Who's a good girl, Tilly?" He took a treat from his pocket and fed it to Tilly. "That's right, you are."

Wow. Tilly and Billy. Interesting. Of course, who was I to talk? I named my girl Smooshie.

"I meant it when I said I loved working here. It's the only job I know where I can bring my girl to work with me. I don't want that to change. I like Waggin' Trails the way it is, but I knew that if it got out, I slept with a guest. A married one at that, I'd probably be fired. Going along with his plan was me stalling for time to come up with my own plan."

"A plan to kill Dade," I said.

Billy's voice grew thin and reedy. "I didn't murder anyone. I swear it."

"Well, hell. I guess that's that." Unfortunately, this meant we were down another suspect because Billy, while foolish, was telling the truth.

"You won't tell on me, will you?"

"I have to tell Deputy Booth," I said bluntly. "You could've gotten Trudy and her husband killed. You know that, right?"

"I know," he whined. "But I didn't mean to. And they're both fine. No harm, no foul."

"Plead your case to the Waddles. Come clean. I'm going to tell Nadine, but if Trudy and Jonathan don't press charges, you stand a chance of not going to jail. I can't say what will happen with your job. Truthfully, though, I can't see you getting out of this without some kind of consequence."

"Hey," I heard Parker say. I looked over my shoulder and saw him walking toward Billy and me.

"Hey, back."

He came up behind me and put his arm over me and across my chest. "I was getting worried about you." He kissed the top of my head. I smiled. Parker wasn't a shifter, but sometimes our mate bond brought out his alpha. "Are you feeling okay?"

"I'm fine, babe." I leaned my head against his shoulder. "Just getting some things straightened out with Billy."

"Are you done? Lunch is at the table."

"Already?"

"They were fast," he said.

I nodded to Billy. "Think about what I said, you know, about the Waddles," I told him. "I think Trudy might be more merciful than you think." I wrinkled my nose and added, "As long as you don't mention anything about Greta, of course."

"Duly noted. And Lily," Billy said. "Thank you."

As Parker and I walked away, he leaned into my ear and said, "What was that about?"

"A boy and his dog," I said cryptically. I'd tell him the rest when we were somewhere private.

"I get that." Parker chuckled. "He had a cute corgi."

I made a face. "Her name is Tilly."

"Billy and Tilly?" he asked incredulously.

"Right?" I laughed. "So weird, but kind of cute."

"Definitely," Parker agreed.

On the way back to the restaurant, I resisted the serious urge to run down the corridor to our hotel room and hug Smooshie and Elvis until the icky feeling I had in the pit of my stomach disappeared.

CHAPTER 16

The lodge, for all its spaciousness, had started to feel like a small box. I don't know if it was the stress of the case or what that had me itching to get out of my skin, but there came a point in the afternoon that I thought my cougar was going to burst right out of me without any warning. The snow had finally stopped, but it didn't look like it was gong to warm up anytime soon.

After lunch, I'd told Nadine about Billy's chair lift sabotage. She said she was going to look into it. When I told Parker, I could tell he was worried about what might happen next. We'd gone back to the room to decompress and check on the dogs, but decompression wasn't in my cards. Elvis was on a pile of blankets near the heating vent while Smooshie had decided that pacing back and forth with me was her new favorite game.

"I'm taking the dogs on a run," I said. "I need to work off this extra energy."

"The snow's still pretty thick out there." Parker sat

on the end of the bed. "It might be more of a slogging than a run."

I pushed back the curtain and stared out across the white landscape. "I don't care if I have to bellycrawl."

"They have treadmills in the gym if you just want to burn some fuel." He held out his hand to me. "I'll go with you if you want."

I took his offered hand and pushed my legs between his open knees. In this position, I was slightly taller than Parker. I tilted his chin up with my free hand and kissed him.

Smooshie leaned into his legs, pushing Parker's knee into my thigh, then she started licking my toes. I crawled up onto Parker's lap, exploring the kiss more as his hands slid down my back to cup my buttocks. He lifted me with one great effort, then flipped me onto the bed.

I squealed, delighted at this literal turn of events. I was pretty sure in make-out terms, I was about to get to second base. "As energy burns go, I rank this one way above running on a treadmill.

Parker rubbed his face against mine before pressing his lips to the area where my earlobes met my neck. The rasp of his afternoon stubble, along with the warmth of his breath on my skin, caused a shiver of pleasure that didn't end until it reached my toes.

"Perhaps we should see if Dad wants to dog sit later, and we can really put all your excess energy to good use," Parker said.

"We should call him right now." I ran a finger down

Parker's chest. "This vacation is starting to look up again."

A bark and a whine from Smooshie barely distracted us, but then she jumped up on the bed and let loose a long squeaky fart near our heads.

"Oh, Goddess." I gagged, rolling away and shoving Parker into the path of the toxic fumes.

Parker choked on a laugh as he tried to get away from Gas-zilla. "I swear it's thick enough to cut," he said. He gave Smooshie a condemning stare as he waved his hand in front of him. "Dang, girl. What have you been eating?"

I was dying now, laughing at Parker. Laughing at Smooshie's intestinal madness. We played keep away as she happily chased us around the room. Elvis stood up, his tail wagging hard, as he barked at all of us. I agreed with him, we were ridiculous, but it was a kind of ridiculous I needed.

I ran to the window and slid it open a crack. The cold breeze shunting into the room was enough to wash the heat of the moment away. Parker came up behind me and put his arms around my waist as we gazed out at the frozen mountain.

"Not what you expected for your first vacation, huh?"

"Not exactly," I replied. "I guess I was hoping this would be a mini-honeymoon for us, you know, since we hadn't done that yet."

"Every day's a honeymoon as long as I'm with you," he told me.

I leaned my head back and smiled wistfully, "I feel

the same. Even so, a weekend without work and responsibility, just all of us enjoying each other's good company, I'd really been looking forward to that."

"I'm sorry, Lily." He kissed the tip of my ear.

"It's not your fault." I reached back and pressed my palm against his cheek. "I blame that scoundrel Maddox for being someone who lots of people wanted dead."

"Who do you think done it?"

"Too early to tell." I shrugged. "Could be any of them. It could be none of them. It sounds as if his work makes for a lot of angry folks. Maybe it's someone who hasn't even been on our radar yet. I could see someone following the jackass here with the intent of killing him."

"It doesn't exactly seem like a professional hit," Parker said.

"No, you're right." I turned in his arms, raising my brow as the chilly wind coming through the window blew up the back of my t-shirt. "But maybe that's the beauty of it. Maybe the killer is proficient at making his or her victims look like an amateur who couldn't murder their way out of a doggy poop bag."

Parker snorted a laugh. "Do you really think that's a possibility?"

I shook my head. "Nope. But I kind of like all the suspects." I shrugged. "Mostly."

"You have a great capacity for empathy, sweet Lily. It's one of the many things I love about you."

"I never doubt you," I said with all seriousness. "I never doubt your love, your faithfulness, our life together.

None of it. I hope you know that I'm aware of how lucky I am to have found you. Smooshie might have rescued me from oncoming traffic the first day we met, but you have rescued me from a lifetime of merely surviving."

He folded me in his arms. "You saved my life, Lily. You saved me."

"We rescued each other," I said.

He chuckled. "It's the family business."

"Come on, Smooshie," I said. "Keep up."

I swear my jubilant girl was stopping to smell her own tracks in the snow as we walked down to the end of the cabins and back. Every few minutes, I'd feel the tug of her leash, and we'd stop so she could plunge her nose into a hole in the snow.

Winter boots made running hard, so I'd turned the outing into a race-walk when Smooshie wasn't sightseeing. Parker had taken Elvis for an indoor walk since both of them preferred the warmer environment. Like Smooshie, though, I needed the fresh air, the sound of the wind rustling through the trees, and nothing overhead but sky, sky, and more sky.

She ran out ahead of me, and the sight of her wiggling butt and swishing tail filled my heart with joy. I was focused on her bouncy steps when Trudy Waddle beckoned my attention.

"Lily," she said loudly, then waved.

I waved back. She was walking her dog Magnus, and

they were coming up on the far side of the road leading away from the lodge.

Smooshie tugged on the leash, trying to move closer to Trudy and her dog. "Heel," I commanded. She'd gotten much better with simple commands over the past year, as long as she wasn't overly excited. Smooshie fell back next to me. I gave her ear a grateful scratch. She was going to get a nice treat when we got back to the lodge. "Good girl."

Trudy's dog, once again, was a perfect gentleman. He barely even glanced in our direction.

"Got to get in that exercise," Trudy said. "Mags is an old boy, but he can still get anxious if he's pent up for too long."

"He's a handsome fella. How long have you had him?"

"Magnus was a search and rescue dog with a Federal Emergency Management System. Jonathan worked for FEMA as his handler. Jonathan's always had a special bond with him, so when FEMA retired Magnus two years ago, Jonathan retired too. He's been living the good life since then." She ran her gloved hand over his scruff. "He saved my life. It's how we met."

"This is a story I need to hear," I said with genuine interest. I couldn't help but feel a connection to Trudy.

"It happened ten months after we lost the court case," she added for context. "My son Paul had gotten engaged to Greta. Her family is from Utah, and she'd wanted the wedding to take place at this beautiful chalet overlooking the mountain range. Long story short, the wedding happened. Paul and Greta absconded off to Fiji for their honeymoon, and I decided to stay a few days. There were forty of us on that hillside when the avalanche crashed down on top of us," Trudy recounted. "Three people died, but the rest of us made it out alive, thanks to the efforts of search and rescue. Jonathan and Magnus found me half-buried and with frostbitten toes. I got lucky that day in that I found two new loves and a second lease on life." She smiled. "Jonathan asked me my name as he dug me out of the snow. I told him Gertrude, and he called me Trudy. Two months later, he married me." She shook her head. "I haven't felt like Gertrude since then...until this weekend. Sometimes history can really bite you in the ass."

"Ain't that the truth," I said, feeling the irony. Smooshie began to shiver. "I better get her back to the lodge. The winter coat only helps for so long in these temperatures."

Trudy smirked. "I've got two missing toes to prove it."

When my eyes widened, she laughed. "I'm sure we'll speak again, Lily. There's something about you that fascinates me."

"Ditto," I told her. "You and Magnus enjoy your walk."

By the time I got Smooshie back up to the lodge, she was good and ready to be indoors again. The lobby was busier than it had been all day. Had the power finally come back on? Or were these angry guests who were organizing a protest. I understood why they were unhappy, but it wasn't like Billy could magically fix the power.

I saw Reggie at a table stacked with water bottles, some kind of bin, and she was holding a clipboard. She gestured for me when I got inside the lobby. She had a look of consternation about her, serious and worried.

"What's wrong?" I asked as Smooshie and I crossed over to her. "Did something happen? Was someone else hurt?"

"We don't know," she said. "Not for certain. It's Cat. She's missing, and Marshall got a frantic and unsettling voicemail from her."

"Saying what?"

"In Cat's message, she told Marshall, someone was trying to kill her."

I blinked at Reggie. "She's in danger. Are there any leads on her whereabouts?"

"We're organizing search parties. No groups smaller than three. Nadine has tasked the groups with searching the lodge from top to bottom, making a grid pattern. Greer, Parker, and Buzz have all joined the search. Billy had a dozen two-way radios in the security shed and enough batteries to get most of them working." She held one up. "I'm checking off sections on the hotel map as they're being cleared."

I saw Jonathan and Paul crossing the lobby. Jonathan had a pair of long skis and ski poles with him. "Where are you going?" Reggie asked.

Jonathan pointed at the exit. "I'm going to find my wife, then the three of us will do a search outside while it's still daylight ."

Before Reggie could protest, I said, "Jonathan worked in search and rescue for FEMA. If anyone's qualified, he is."

Paul held up two pairs of snowshoes and a backpack. "We have water, food, and warming blankets, along with fire-making supplies and other items, if we get caught out there."

Jonathan gave his son-in-law an approving nod. "I worked rescue for a long time. Let me do what I know how to do," he said to Reggie. "If Cat's out there, I can help."

"Fine," Reggie said. She grabbed a walkie-talkie from the table. "Take this. We're on channel six. The range is only good for two miles. Try not to go any farther than that. If you see anything, radio back. If you run into anyone who is or isn't Cat or someone you know, don't approach them. Radio back. And if you get into trouble...."

Jonathan took the two-way and held it up. "Got it. I'll radio back."

"We have to find her," I told my friend. I'd been planning to check on Cat this evening. I was kicking myself for not doing it earlier. I'd never considered that she could be a target like her husband. "She has to be safe."

CHAPTER 17

I joined Parker and Greer on the interior search. Room after room, there was no sign of Cat Maddox anywhere. Our section of the grid included the room with Dade's corpse. Reggie had done that on purpose, to prevent the other guests from further contaminating the body.

"Damn," Greer said when we unlocked the door. "This room is freezing."

The windows were wide open, and the vents, as Nadine had said, were covered and taped off. Dade's body was on top of a large piece of plastic, like what painters used to protect the floor that had been laid over the mattress, and there was a sheet crumpled up at the foot of the bed.

"I covered Maddox's body when we put him here last night," Parker said. "It must've slid off."

I noticed Dade's shirt had several new holes in the front that hadn't been there before. "That's strange." I glanced over at the window. There was a corner of the screen flapping as a stiff breeze blew in. I walked over and lifted the flap. The cut extended up one side and across the bottom, creating an opening big enough for someone to crawl through.

"Christ in a Cracker Barrel," Greer swore. "Is that what I think it is?"

Parker had seen the holes as well. Carefully, using the antenna on the radio, he lifted Dade's shirt. There were puncture wounds, six of them, on the dead man's sternum, ribs, and abdomen. "It looks like someone crawled in through the window and decided to make sure dead meant dead." He shook his head. "What kind of a person does this?"

The wounds were uneven but not frantic.

"I think it was someone who was making sure they'd finished the job," I said.

Greer's lip raised in a snarl. "Someone insane, if they couldn't tell he was dead already."

"Do you see any footprints outside?" Parker asked.

The room was on the mountain view side of the lodge, and the snow was still too cold to pack, so any evidence of tracks had been efficiently covered or blown away.

"Nothing," I told him. "Just a lot of winter." I closed both windows and locked them. Hopefully, with the room as cold as it was and the vents covered, the temperature wouldn't rise much. Either way, it was the only way to ensure that the killer didn't come back through this way.

"Do you think when he took Cat that he dragged her out this window?" Greer asked.

"I don't know." I had no clue at this point what the heck was happening. The clues to this murder pointed to everyone and no one. How was that even possible? "I want to listen to the voicemail she left Marshall. Maybe I'll hear something in the background. Something, you know... something that might have been missed by normal ears."

"Good plan," Parker said. He held the radio in front of his face. "Reggie, do you copy? This is Parker."

"Parker, I copy," Reggie said. "What do you have for me?"

"Section seven is clear, but you're going to want to hand off your station to someone else and head down to room eighty-nine."

There was a pause, then Reggie said, "Isn't that...." She let the question hang.

"Roger that," Parker confirmed. "Evidence has been compromised."

"Ask her about Marshall," I said.

"Can we get a location on Marshall?" Parker asked.

"He's in the watchtower at the top of the ski slope. It's a good birds' eye view," Reggie said. "Do you need him to come back to the lodge?"

I shook my head. "I can go to him."

"Not alone, you don't," Greer said.

I reached out and took my father-in-law's hand. "I'll be fine," I told him. "But if it makes you feel better, you can come with me."

"It would make me feel better." He scratched his head. "I know you're special, but that doesn't stop me from worrying about you."

"I'd be hurt if you did."

Parker nodded to me. "You two go ahead. I'll wait for Reggie."

He knew as well as I did that seconds and minutes counted when someone was missing. And from what Parker had told me, Greer understood as well.

"Then it's settled. Greer and I will head up to the watchtower."

"Be safe," Parker said. "I'll see you soon."

GREER AND I BOTH PUT ON OUR SNOW GEAR, GOT some snowshoes from Billy, and made our way to the watchtower. It was located a good fifty yards up the mountain from the slopes, and I could feel the air thinning.

"Are you okay?" I asked Greer.

"Fine," he huffed. "We're almost there."

He was in great shape and nowhere near being geriatric, so I took him at his word. The tower had a long ladder climb of at least forty rungs.

"This is going to be fun," Greer grumbled.

"One rung after another. It's easy as that," I teased.

"As easy," he agreed. "And as hard."

If he'd been out of breath before, by the time we got to the hatch, he was gasping. I was struggling myself. I wasn't used to the high altitude, and it was taking its toll on my body.

I knocked on the hatch. Marshall opened it then

gave me a hand up. After I was in, he and I both pulled Greer inside.

"Have you heard anything?" Marshall asked.

I'd known he had been worried for Cat before, but now, I could see that his feelings went deeper. Did he love Cat? Was he infatuated or obsessed? I shook the feeling of foreboding away. Even if he was, she'd left the message for Marshall. He couldn't have been the man she was afraid of. Right?

"Nothing yet," I quickly told him after I tugged off my face covering. "I'm sure they'll send word as soon as any new developments happen. Can I listen to the recording Cat left you?"

"Sure." He opened his phone and tapped the voice mail. "Here it is."

I took off my gloves and took the phone from him. I pushed play.

Oh...Oh, God. He's angry. So angry. She sounded disoriented and scared. Her fear made my stomach hurt. *He wants to kill me,* she continued. There was a delay of a few seconds, then she said, *Help me. Please help.*

"We have to find her," Marshall said. "She's counting on me."

"We'll do our best." Greer patted the young man's shoulder. He gave me an encouraging smile. "And our best is very good."

"Do you have earbuds or, better yet, headphones?" I asked Marshall. "It will help me isolate background noises."

"Don't you need a computer program for that?"

Greer shook his head. "Lily has excellent ears."

I nodded my agreement. "What he said."

"I have some noise-canceling headphones." He pushed the power button on the side and handed me a neon green set. "They're synced to my phone already. I like to wear them when I *shred the gnar*."

"I'll take your word for it," I said. "Thanks." I put the headphones on and was amazed how eerily quiet everything became. "That's so weird."

Marshall gave me a crooked smile and two thumbs up before grabbing his binoculars and going to the window to search for Cat.

There was a small space heater in the watchtower, but to say the structure was warm would be overstating it by a lot. I put one of my gloves back on and used my non-gloved hand to push the play button. I listened over and over. There was something in the pause. Faint, but there. It could've been an ambient noise, but there was a pattern. I closed my eyes so that Marshall wouldn't see my cougar slip into them, and I focused on sharpening my hearing.

Oh...Oh, God. He's angry. So angry. He wants to kill me .... Help me. Please help.

During the pause, I heard the pattern again. This time more distinctively. *Click. Click. Clickity-click.* It continued in the background and was repeating. As I listened to it one more time, I realized where I knew the pattern. It had been the watch on Cat and Dade's dresser.

I leaped to my feet. "She was in the cabin." I took off the headphones. "Cabin seven. We have to get over there Now."

Greer used the two-way to call back to the lodge. "Did you find anything?" Nadine answered.

"Lily is sure the message originated in cabin number seven. She recognized a sound in the background," Greer informed her.

"We'll get someone down there right away," Nadine responded.

"I'm close," a man said over the radio. "I'll go check it out."

"Who is this?" Nadine asked.

"It's Jonathan Waddle. Paul and I are still looking for Trudy, but I'm not far from Cabin seven. I'll go down and take a look."

"Wait for someone to get there, Jonathan," Nadine warned.

He didn't answer her.

"Jonathan," she said sharply. "Tell me you copy."

Again, there was no answer.

"The snowmobile," Marshall said. "We can get there in a few minutes if we go now." I could tell the guy was itching with worry.

I glanced over at Greer. "I'm going," I said. "Are you going to be okay with that?"

"No," he replied. He handed me the radio. "Be safe."

"I will." I went up on my tiptoes and kissed his cheek. "Thanks, Dad."

Greer's expression softened at my term of endearment. "Go," he said. "Before I change my mind. I'll keep an eye out up here."

I put my face covering back on, along with the glove.

Marshall pointed to a console. There's a radio if you see anything. It doesn't cross over with the walkie-talkies, but it will connect you to the lodge."

"Lily," Greer said. "If you see danger, run the other way."

I clapped his shoulder. "Wise words to live by."

"The keyword, there," he said, "is live."

I pocketed the radio and slid down the ladder as if my butt was on fire, and the only thing that could put it out was getting to the bottom. Of course, then I had to wait for Marshall to come down.

When he reached the ground, he said, "Man, that was the fastest I've ever seen anyone descend. Are you a fireman?"

"Nope." Just a werecougar on a mission. "Where's the snowmobile?"

"It's in a shed off to the side of the hot chocolate shack."

"Cool." I gestured for him to keep up. "Let's go."

CHAPTER 18

We quickly retrieved the snowmobile and set off for the cabins. Using a shortcut through the woods, Marshall delivered us to Cabin 7 in just a few minutes as promised. I had the impression he'd made that trip more than once before. I spotted Buzz's SUV parked out front, and my adrenaline kicked up a notch. Was Cat still inside? Had they found her? Was she alive?

I felt sick to my gut as I hopped off the snowmobile and rushed to the open front door. "Did you find her?" I asked before I even saw anyone. "Is she in there?"

Parker met me at the door. He had blood on his jacket.

"Is she..." I couldn't finish the sentence.

"No," he said. "It's not her blood."

"Then whose?"

"You're going to be all right, sweetheart," I heard Jonathan say. "Help is on the way."

I hurried by Parker. Trudy was on the dining room

floor, Jonathan cradled her head, and Buzz was putting pressure on the wound.

"We've called Reggie. She's gathering medical supplies, and I was just on my way to go get her and bring her down," Parker said.

"What happened? Is she going to be okay?"

Parker nodded. "I think so. I've seen worse wounds. Whoever did it, stabbed her in the outer edge of her abdomen, and there was an exit wound directly out her back. I don't think it got her intestines or any major organs. Jonathan says when he got to the cabin, the door was open, and he saw Trudy on the kitchen floor. No one else was inside. At least not that he saw."

"Has Trudy said anything. Did she see who did this?"

"She's out of it." Parker gave me a look that said this whole situation was over his paygrade. "It's like she's been drugged."

Another thought hit me. "Magnus. He was with her when she was on her walk. Is he okay?"

"He wouldn't have left Trudy's side," Jonathan said. "Not unless she ordered him, too."

"Go," I said to Parker. "Go get Reggie."

He gave me a quick kiss and left.

Marshall raced into the cabin. "Cat!" he shouted. "Cat, where are you?"

"She's not here," I said. "But we'll find her." I hoped I wasn't lying. I prayed whoever did this to Trudy wasn't planning worse for the fragile woman.

The kitchen grew quiet, and I heard a slight whimper followed by a whine somewhere in the cabin. I tracked the noise down the hall to the master bedroom.

The bathroom door was closed, but I heard the whine again. "It's okay," I said. "I'm going to open the door now."

When I cracked the door to peek in, Magnus stood at the back near the shower. He growled.

"No, no. It's okay," I said. Then I heard the whimper again. It wasn't Magnus. It was Milo. The smaller dog was behind the Malinois, and it seemed that he'd found his champion in Magnus. They were safe. I closed the door and let out a sigh of relief.

"Magnus is okay," I shouted. "He's in the bathroom with Milo. It looks like they were shut inside to get them out of the way."

I pulled the curtain back in the kitchen and looked out the window. "Where's Paul?" I asked Jonathan. Trudy's son had been with him when they went to look for her.

Jonathan shook his head. "He saw something in the woods and took off. I couldn't stop him."

Terrific. Now we had two missing persons. "Where did he see the movement?"

Jonathan stared at me. "He was looking out the window, so from that direction. Foolish man. I tried to stop him, but he wouldn't listen to me. And...and I couldn't leave Trudy."

"Reggie will be here soon." I understood how Jonathan felt. If it had been Parker lying on the floor, stabbed, and drugged, I wouldn't have left him either. She's the best doctor I know. And she's a surgeon, so she'll know precisely what Trudy will need."

Buzz glanced at me. "Nadine has the kids. I'll have

to go after Reggie gets here and take over for her. Are you okay?"

I no longer knew. "I think so." Don't cry, I told myself. Do. Not. Cry. I took a deep breath, and when I looked out the curtain again, I saw someone crawling out of the woods in the snow. The person looked up, pain and desperation on her face. "It's Cat," I said. "Oh, my gosh. It's Cat."

Excitedly, I sprinted out of the cabin. Marshall was right on my heels. "Cat!" I yelled. "We're coming."

She collapsed into the snow. I was there first, but Marshall was a close second. We lifted Cat to her feet. Her bottom lip was swollen, and she had a bruise next to her right eye. There was also blood on her coat.

"Are you injured?" I asked as I checked her over.

"No," she said. "I…I killed him. I think I…."

"The man who did this," I said. "Where is he?"

She pointed out into the woods. "I stabbed him," Cat said. She sounded like she was in shock. "I just kept stabbing."

"It's okay," I told her. "You did what you had to do. Are you sure he's dead?"

"I think so." Her quiet voice sounds small and frightened. "I'll…I'll show you. It's not far."

"We should get you back to the cabin. I'll go find the body after."

"It's not far," she said. "Just over the ravine. I pushed him in."

"Okay," I said. "But you stay back with Marshall. If for some reason he's still alive, I want you safe."

"Yeh…yes," she agreed. "I'll stay safe."

I had the radio in my jacket. I took it out and pressed the button. "I found Cat," I said. "She says she subdued her attacker. He's dead. I'm going to check it out."

"Not alone," Nadine came back.

"I've got Cat and Marshall. Cat says the suspect is at the bottom of a ravine. If that's true, I think I'm safe." I felt almost giddy. Even so, I couldn't shake this nagging feeling that wouldn't stop tickling my subconscious. "About how far?"

"Not far," Cat said. "I need to see for myself. I need to know he's finally dead."

Marshall had his arm around her. "You're safe now, Cat. No one will ever hurt you again, I swear."

"That's nice," she told him. They stayed about fifteen feet behind me as I led the way to the ravine. The ravine, it turned out, was a large sinkhole in the mountain that was twenty feet across and at least that many feet high. There was a large pool of water covered in a clear layer of ice, taking up most of the basin. Based on how much time it took to get there, I guesstimated the gigantic hole was less than a quarter mile from the edge of the woods in a northeasterly direction.

I saw a body lying face down at the bottom near the water's edge. The legs were twisted into an unwieldy position, and he wasn't moving. "I pretty sure you got him, Cat. He won't ever try to hurt you again." I looked back to give Cat a reassuring smile, and my mouth dropped open in horror.

Cat Maddox, a woman I'd only been able to see as a victim, held a large, bloody knife in her hands.

"Marshall," I said.

"Lily?" Marshall's palms were pressed to his stomach, his face contorted with disbelief. "Lily," he said again. Blood sprayed as he coughed. The stab wound had hit his lung. Marshall went down to his knees and fell over.

"Cat?" I asked. "What are you doing?"

"He's a demon," she said. "No matter how many times I kill him, he won't die. I finally fought back. I hit him, and he went down. He was dead. But then, two hours later, he was alive again. That's when I knew he was possessed. He acted like he didn't remember what happened, but he was even more angry than usual."

"Dade?" I asked. "Are you talking about Dade?"

"And then at the party. I gave him what should have been enough of my medicine to kill him, but still, he didn't die. Then the lights went out. So, I killed him again."

"Did you climb into the window of his room?" I asked.

"I had to," she told me. "He wasn't dead, so I stabbed him again. Then he found me in the woods." She looked down at Marshall. "And now he's found me again."

"No," I told her. It was evident Cat was having some kind of psychotic break. "That's Marshall. Your friend, Marshall. He's been so worried about you."

She shook her head and held up the knife. I saw that her fingers were red and swollen, the beginnings of frostbite. I held up my hand. "Put the knife down, and I'll make sure you get some help."

The radio in my pocket came to life. It was Reggie's voice. "Lily, do you copy?"

"I need to answer that," I told Cat.

"Don't," she ordered, stepping forward with the knife pointed at me. "I don't want to hurt you."

Marshall groaned and said, "Oh, God."

"Shut up," Cat snapped. "Why won't you die?" she screamed. "How many times do I have to kill you before you stay dead?"

"Lily, are you there? Pick up?" Reggie said again.

"Reggie's a doctor," I said. "She can help you, Cat. She can help you and Marshall."

"No one can help me," she said. "I'm marked." She held up her wrist and pointed to her scar with the tip of the blade. "The beast will never let me go. I have to defend myself."

What could I say to that revelation? "I'll help you. I'll help you fight him."

"You're lying," she said. "I can tell when people are lying."

That hit a little too close to home. Marshall struggled to his knees, trying to get away, but his shallow wheezing meant he was struggling to breathe.

Cat screamed. She raised her hand, ready to swing the blade into Marshall's neck.

I let out a scream of my own, but this one was my werecougar. When Cat looked at me, she staggered back a few feet. "Demon," she hissed. "Beast. You're one of them."

"Lily, if you can hear me," Reggie said. "Cat is on an antidepression drug called esketamine. It's a form of ketamine—a hypnotic drug that can cause disassociation, delusions, and hallucinations. It's for patients with depression who have suicidal thoughts and are resistant to other depression drugs."

This would've been great information to know twenty minutes earlier.

"Keep your distance if you can. Trudy is coming around, and she says that Cat is the one who attacked her. Trudy said she fought back, but that's when Cat sprayed the medication several times in Trudy's face to subdue her."

Now it was all starting to make sense.

"Cat, let me help you," I said. "I'm going to slowly take the radio from my pocket."

"I can't let you live," she said. "Not again."

And that's when she rushed me. As she crashed into me, the weight of her body sent us both over the side of the steep chasm and into the icy water below.

CHAPTER 19

I regained consciousness with icy water surrounding me. It took me a few seconds to remember that I had taken a twenty-foot dive off a cliff. The impact of our bodies must've broken the ice. Luckily, the water wasn't deep. Still, my arms and legs were a combination of intense pain and numbness that comes with a plunge into freezing waters.

My head and back hurt, but I could move. I counted that as a good sign. Shifters healed quicker than humans, but a severed spinal cord or a broken neck would take more magic than any human surgeon could muster.

I got up on my elbow and saw Cat was lying next to me in the water. She was breathing but unconscious, and her lips were turning blue.

"Cat," I said. "Cat, wake up." Was she dangerous? Absolutely. But she was also suffering from a severe mental illness, which meant she needed my help, not my condemnation. But she wasn't the only one who needed me. Marshall was up top, bleeding to death. Marshall first, I told myself. Then Cat.

I got to my feet and shoved my hand into my wet jacket pocket. The walkie-talkie was still there. If I could radio for help, I might be able to save all of us. I had a moment of hope until nothing happened when I pressed down on the button.

I bellowed my frustration. The water had damaged my only hope of getting help fast. Was Marshall even alive? I had no idea how long it had been since I'd fallen. The sun set at seven-thirty, and it was still light out. It couldn't have been that much time since Cat had taken us both over the edge. "Marshall!"

There was no answer. "Marshall!" I shouted again. "If you can hear me, say something. I'm listening." I stretched my hearing. Still nothing. The sides of the sinkhole were made of smooth rock, and it went up and curled in like an arch. With the pain and numbness in my fingers, there was no way I'd be able to climb out, and my cougar would be even less adept at scaling the sheer, curved wall.

I saw who the dead man was and my heart sunk. Paul Michaels, Trudy's son. Raged burned inside me at his senseless death. Trudy had already lost so much with her daughter, but to lose her son also was suffering beyond what anyone should have to experience. I reigned in my anger. It wouldn't do Paul any good at this point, and I had to focus on getting Cat to somewhere dry, or she would die of hypothermia. I remembered Paul had taken a survival bag with him. I walked over, sickened at the sight of his contorted legs and waxy complexion, and searched for the bag. I found it ten feet away in the water.

"I'm sorry," I said to him. "I promise I'll be back for you."

I knew, eventually, my family would find me. They knew I was missing, and they also knew the general direction. But until the rescue came, I had to do my best to survive. I glanced over at Cat. I had to keep us both alive.

I dragged Cat from the water onto the snow. Regrettably, it was deep on the edges, so there wasn't any reprieve from the cold. I knew I had to get her wet clothes off, but I needed to find us a shelter of some kind first.

I found two mylar rescue blankets in the backpack. I grabbed one. It took me a few minutes to open the cellophane wrapping, but I finally managed. I unfolded the silver sheet and put it over Cat, tucking the edges behind her so the blanket would stay put. After, I walked down along the frozen edges, searching for a miracle. Instead, I found a hollow in the side of the wall. It was a shallow cave that went back five feet or so. I threw the backpack inside the covered space. The numbness in my limbs affected my ability to walk and even think. There was only one way to survive the cold, and it wasn't in my human form. It took multiple tries and a lot of fumbling, but I finally got my coat off. My teeth chattered as I shed the rest of my clothing.

Between the hypothermia and the brain fog, I had difficulty bringing about the shift. I was not separate from my cougar side, but it was as if there was some kind of disconnect. I'd been disconnected from that side of me before, after a head injury. Maybe, that's what was happening now. I couldn't let myself think that way. If I did, I'd lose hope, and hope kept people alive.

"Please," I said to my other half. "This is no time to be shy."

I shook my hands and bounced on the balls of my feet. It was not helping. If I couldn't shift, I knew I'd succumb to the freezing temperatures. My internal core was the only thing that kept me moving at this point, but I could feel that strength dwindling by the second. It was as if the cold had frozen my animal inside me.

My fingers were turning to sausages. I blinked at my wedding band. Parker. I had to live. I couldn't let this situation beat me. I'd do anything to get back to him, and I knew that included my cougar half. I stilled my mind to control the rising panic, so I could try and clear my mind and reach my animal side. Parker was her mate. Our mate. We were bonded in every way, so I called on that bond to stir her from whatever it was inside me that kept her locked away.

I reached out with my thoughts, searching every part of my mind for where she could be hiding. Then suddenly, she was there. I inhaled deeply, the cold constricting my lungs, then let out a stuttering breath and concentrated on my bones. I willed them to bend, to break, and to reform. I felt my skin give way as fur sprouted down my body. My hands and feet turned to paws, and my long torso turned into a sleek blonde body that was made for stealth and speed. The elation of shifting brought a roar to my lips that was distinctly sharp and thunderous.

I shook my wedding band from my clawed front toes then loped out of the cave. Using my teeth, I bit into the shoulder fabric of Cat's coat and dragged her across the snow and into the cave. I went back for the silver mylar. When I returned to Cat, I was already so much warmer under thick winter fur. The feeling had returned to my limbs, so I risked turning again.

I shifted back to my naked human self and let out a squeak as the bitter cold hit all my nooks and crannies. "Holy crap," I gasped. Warming up in a fur coat had brought life back to my body, and Mother Nature was making sure I felt every bit of it.

I was relieved to see the swelling in my fingers wasn't nearly as bad as it had been. I made quick work undressing Cat. Her breathing was shallow, and her pulse had slowed significantly. I knew if I didn't warm her up, her lungs and brain would be compromised.

I danced around, shivering as I got the other rescue blanket from the backpack. I was glad that some of my dexterity had returned, but in my human form, I had to hurry, or I was going to be useless again. I shook the folded blanket out and laid it on the ground. I undressed Cat then and pulled her on top of it. I was familiar with how to treat severe hypothermia. The key was increasing core temperature. I searched the backpack for anything that could become a heat source. I celebrated when I discovered four of those hand warmers people tucked into mittens in a side pocket. My teeth were chattering again as I activated the packs and put two under her armpits, one on her groin and one behind her neck.

Goddess, it was so cold. "You can do this, Lily," I told myself. "You're not the give up and die type." I recalled Trudy's words, how she believed that survivors were the kind of people who were strong even without life crapping on them. Then Gloria Gaynor's song popped into my head, and I hummed it while I finished wrapping Cat like a tin foil burrito.

When I finished taking care of Cat, I gobbled an energy bar from the backpack and drank a six-ounce sports drink. The calories would help keep my temperature up. "Thank you, Paul," I sent out into the world. My chest squeezed, thinking about him just outside the cave. No longer alive because life sometimes had a way of kicking you in the teeth. Was this the other shoe I'd stopped waiting for? No, stop it. I wouldn't think that way.

Cat moaned but didn't wake up. The pocket heaters were helping, but it wasn't enough to stave off below zero temperatures. I was going to have to risk further exposing my true nature.

I partially put the second blanket over Cat's bundled body and then lay down next to her. I missed Parker and Smooshie and Elvis, and I focused on warm thoughts of being in a puppy pile with the three of them. I grabbed the mylar sheet and brought it over my shoulder, then put my arm over Cat's chest and breathed.

Slowly, I shifted until my large cougar was once more in my place. My chest rumbled as I purred loudly.

It was so lovely to be warm again. I snuggled against Cat. Between the heat packs, the mylar swaddle, and a one-hundred-and-ten-pound fur generator, I prayed it would be enough. We just needed to hold on for a little while. I'd expended so much energy helping Cat, and now that I was somewhat warm again, I struggled to keep my eyes open.

"Hello," I heard a woman say.

I blinked my eyes open and saw Cat staring at me.

"You're so pretty," she said. "You're an angel."

I looked down my nose at her. Crap. I still had whiskers.

Cat's nose had started to turn a dark blue, but she was talking. That was a good sign. The fact that she was talking to a cougar and not freaking out, well, I'm not sure what that said about her mental state. At least, she wasn't accusing me of being a demon. I held still because I didn't want to startle her.

"Am I dead?" she asked. "Is this heaven?"

I purred because, well, I wasn't sure what the alternative would be.

She poked her bruised fingers from the neck of the wrap and scratched my chin. I took some exception to that and snarled. Cat tucked her hand back inside.

"Okay," she said. "No touching." She closed her eyes. "If you get hungry, don't eat Milo, okay? Take me instead because I'm already dead."

Whoa. I held very still as she drifted back to sleep.

"Lily!" I heard Parker roar. "Lily!" His tone was frantic and demanding. "Answer me."

I let out a growl that sounded like a crack of thunder. Dang, it. Still in cougar form.

Even so, I heard Parker let out a triumphant shout. "She's down here," he said. "She's alive."

I shifted back to human. I was alive. I'd made it. I pressed my hand to Cat's throat. Her pulse was much more robust. I'd kept her alive as well. "In here," I said, but it came out as a scratchy rasp. I coughed and cleared my throat. "In here," I tried again. This time my voice was clear. Parker, wearing a harness, clambered around the corner, and when I saw him, hot tears streamed down my face.

"I found you," he said, falling to the ground next to me. He pulled me into his arms. "Thank God I found you."

I nodded my head. "I never doubted that you would."

He kissed my face. He was crying too, and it made me cry even harder. "I was so scared, Lily. I've never been so scared in all my life. But I knew you wouldn't leave me. Not after it took so long for you to find me."

"Marshall?" I asked.

Parker smiled. "He's alive. Search and rescue are medevacking him out on a chopper."

The tightness in my chest eased, but I couldn't stop crying. "How did you find me?"

"Smooshie." He shook his head. "She's up top with Greer. I knew she'd lead me right to you. That girl has been tracking you since the day you met."

I laughed, but the tears kept coming.

"Where's the kitty," Cat asked as she roused once again from her sleep.

I shrugged as Parker arched his brow at me and chuckled.

"We found another one," I heard someone say. I think he's got a pulse. It's faint, but it's there."

"Paul," I said. "I thought...." Relief and joy turn my crying into one of those ugly choking sobs.

"When we get you out of here, the helicopter is going to take you to the hospital. There's not enough room for me, but I'll meet you there."

"The roads," I protested.

"I'll plow them myself if I have to." He pressed his forehead to mine. "I love you, Lily."

Two men with rescue cradles, the kind they haul injured people up mountains with, came around the corner. "Need another MOB cradle down here. We have two more live ones."

"Let's get you out of here," Parker said. He scooped me up from the ground.

"Wait," I said, scrambling from his arms. I pushed the mylar aside and frantically searched the ground.

"What are you looking for? Lily," he said when I didn't answer.

Finally, my hand found purchase. "Got it!" I held up my wedding band. "I couldn't leave this behind." I slipped it onto my finger. "Through sunshine and rain."

He shook his head and smiled. "How about after this, we do a little more sunshine and a lot less rain. Or, in this case, snow."

I wrapped the rescue blanket around my chest as I stood up and threw my arms around his neck. I kissed him and replied, "Deal."

CHAPTER 20

I woke up in the hospital at four in the morning with Parker asleep on the couch by the window. "You made it," I said.

He opened his eyes, a half-smile tugging the corner of his lips. "Yep."

"You didn't actually plow the roads, did you?"

He sat up. "Jonathan Waddle called in some favors with his FEMA buddies, and he got a helicopter to take us both off the mountain."

"How is Trudy?" I asked.

"She's doing well. I was right. No, internal organ or intestinal damage. She's going to be right as rain."

"And Paul?"

His mouth thinned in a grim line. "It's a wait and see, right now. The doctors are hopeful. He's going to lose some toes. Trudy says they'll have matching feet then."

I sent up good thoughts for Paul. Trudy needed a win. Frankly, so did I.

"Before you ask," Parker said. "Marshall is expected to make a full recovery. And Cat, well, she might lose the tip of her nose, but otherwise, the doctors think she'll be okay too."

"How did you get all the low down so fast? Are you hanging out with the nurses while I'm asleep?"

He chuckled. "Reggie. She rode up on the helicopter with Trudy as medical support. She's been going back and forth between everyone all night." He gave me a nod. "Including you. You slept pretty hard once the hospital got your temperature back up to normal."

"When can we go home?" After the past two days, I wanted nothing more than to be in my own house and in my own bed.

"Reggie says she'll make sure your lab results don't read anything unusual, and we should be able to go late morning early afternoon. The transportation department promised they'd have the road cleared first thing today, so Dad will drive my truck with the dogs. Nadine is driving the 'Burb with the triplets, and Buzz is taking Dad's truck. It's going to be a circus, but they'll get here."

"Good. I'm done with vacations. Way overrated."

"Couldn't agree more," Parker said. "Besides, every day I get to spend with you is all the vacation I need."

I groaned and rolled my eyes. "Such a cornball."

"I'm your cornball," he amended.

"Damn right." I rolled onto my side. "I can't believe this all started because some jerk was trying to get the owners to sell the place. Well, sort of." Dade Maddox had been the kind of guy that could've gotten himself killed for a multitude of reasons. "Do you think after all this, the Waggin' Trails will get sold?"

"Nadine called the owners last night. Regardles of what happens, Billy Brandish will be in need of another job. They told him to clear out as soon as the weather cleared." Parker waved his hand. "Of course, Nadine told him to stay close. If Trudy and Jonathan decide to press charges, Billy is in a world of hurt."

"He slept with a guest...a married one at that." I held up a finger, "And then he almost killed that guest's mother-in-law," I said. I felt sorry for Tilly, the corgi, but for Billy I had a lot less sympathy. "If losing his job is all that happens to him, he should count himself lucky."

"The local police are going to talk to Trudy about pressing charges," Parker said.

I didn't ask him about Greta. I assumed since she had nothing to do with Dade's murder, Nadine would never have to explain the half-chewed illicit photos. I hoped her husband Paul made a full recovery, but whatever happened between him and his wife would no longer be part of the public record and none of my business.

There was one person I was yet to ask about, because I had mixed feelings about the answer. "What do you think's going to happen to Cat?"

"She told Reggie that she remembers everything, but it's like she was a passenger, not the driver. I guess Paul told her that Dade was responsible for them losing the class action suit. Cat said it brought up all kinds of painful memories, so she took her medicine, only several times higher than her normal dose because it made the pain stop. Then she just kept using it every time she'd start to feel something."

"Why did she attack Trudy?"

"Trudy had found Cat in the cabin, acting out of her mind. She put the dogs in the bathroom for their safety, and that's when Cat attacked her." He pointed to his face. "Cat's black eye and busted lip were from Trudy. She might be twice Cat's age, but Trudy put up a hell of a fight."

"That doesn't surprise me," I told him. "Trudy is a born fighter. Anything else?"

Parker grimaced. "Cat also mentioned something about a large cougar saving her life, but she's pretty sure it was one of her delusions."

I raised my brows. "Oh, yeah. That. It was the only way to save us both."

"And I'm grateful," Parker said. "Reggie thinks she's got a good chance of making an insanity plea work."

"I can attest to her mental state," I said. "I hope she gets the help she needs."

"I don't really care what happens to her, truth be told." Parker got up from the couch. "But I'll support whatever you decide." He climbed into bed next to me. I cradled myself against his chest, relishing in the steady beat of his heart.

"What about Smooshie and Elvis?"

Parker encircled me in his arms and pulled me close. "They are having a sleepover with the Ferrars and loving it. Well, Smooshie is. Elvis is tolerating it." He kissed the top of my head. "Get some sleep, okay. Reggie said it will do your body good to rest."

"I can think of a few other things that would do the body good," I said.

Parker snorted a laugh. "Like a couple of double cheeseburgers and a large, malted shake."

I grinned. "You know me so well."

IN THE MORNING, I HAD SENT PARKER OUT FOR SOME food because I was starving, and I hadn't expected any news other than when I was getting out. But life has a way of doing the opposite of what you expect. Reggie had come in to see me about ten minutes after Parker left to discuss one of my results. Now, I struggled to process what she'd told me about my condition.

There was a knock on the door, then Parker came inside. He held up two bags from Burger Bonanza Emporium. "I got you four double bacon cheeseburgers, two fries, extra ranch, extra mayo, and two fried apple pies."

"Thanks." I smiled wanly, but I couldn't make it reach my eyes. Even so, I didn't have the heart to tell him I'd lost my appetite. "You just missed Reggie. She came in to give me my test results." I patted the bed. "Come sit by me."

He frowned as he set down the bags on the overbed table. "I knew I shouldn't have left." He sat down and took my hand. "Everything's all right, right? I mean, they didn't find anything bad."

I took a deep breath and held it for a second. I was still processing my own feelings. Regardless of how we'd planned to spend the rest of our lives, I knew Parker would be supportive. And while I couldn't magically tell when he was withholding the truth, I knew my guy well enough to read his expressions.

"Lily," he said. "Just rip the bandage off, darling. Whatever it is, we'll get through it." He squeezed my hand. "Together."

I swallowed hard, my throat tight and hot. "I'm pregnant."

Parker stared at me, and I'm pretty sure he stopped breathing for a moment. He definitely didn't blink. "I thought you couldn't get pregnant because of the whole shifter-human thing."

I shrugged. "I shouldn't have been able to form a mate bond with you either," I said. "I have a feeling it's the witch in my family rearing its ugly head again."

"And how do you feel about this new, uhm, development."

"I think it explains a lot of the emotional upheavals I've been experiencing lately." I touched my boobs. "It also explains why these have been a bit sore."

He gave me a crooked smile. "I should feel them and make sure."

"How do you feel about it?" I asked. "Having a baby, I mean. Not my boobs. I know how you feel about them. But kids, that wasn't something we planned for."

"You're right," he said. "It wasn't." His eyes softened. "But, darling, if you tell me you're happy, then I will tell you that I'm the happiest man in the world, and every word of it will be true. I never saw having kids as part of my future, but having our baby, damn, woman, I can't see a future without him…or her." He nodded. "If that's what you want."

"I do," I said. "I want it so much." Which was so strange considering I had sworn to never have kids after being a single teenage mom and raising my brother by myself. I started to cry again. "Damn it. I'm happy, Parker. I'm so freaking happy."

He wrapped his arms around me and hugged me. When I looked up into his blue eyes, he had tears of his own. "Wow, Lily Mason. I never expected you."

"I never expected you, Parker Knowles."

He wiped his eyes with the back of his hand. "I have my own little surprise for you," he said. "It's not as big as yours, but I think you'll like it."

"Well, don't leave me in suspense."

Parker got up and strolled across the room to the door. He opened it up and said, "You all can come in now."

Buzz, Nadine, the triplets, Greer, Reggie, and four gorgeous pit bulls filed into the room.

"Smooshie!" I *squeeed*. "How?" My loveable boop slid around on the tiled floor as she raced to the bed but then managed to make the leap to my lap.

"The hospital allows visits from pets," Reggie said.

"Excellent," I said. I threw my arms around Smooshie and took a good whiff of her fur. "Now it all feels right."

Buzz took a peek at my burger bags, so I smacked his hand away. "Mine," I told him.

He laughed. "I can see you're back in fighting form. Good to see it." His expression relaxed. He'd been worried about me.

"I'm fine," I told him. They all formed a makeshift line, passing out hugs and kisses left and right. It was wonderful. It was family.

Reggie gave me a meaningful look, and I grinned. I could see her relief as well.

Nadine gave my shoulder a quick jab. "Quite the drama," she said ruefully. "What are you planning as an encore?"

I pivoted my gaze sideways to Parker, then back to Nadine, and said, "I think I'll have a baby."

The End... for now.

EARTH SPELLS ARE EASY
GRIMOIRES OF A MIDDLE-AGED WITCH BOOK 1

As a forty-three-year-old, newly divorced, single mom, I know two things for certain, starting over sucks, and magic isn't real. At least that's what I thought. I mean, starting over really does

stink, but when it comes to magic, I have to rethink everything.

I've spent the last year since my ex left me going through the motions. Get up. Work. Care for a grumpy teenager. Cook dinner. Go to bed. Wash. Rinse. Repeat.

Nothing changes... Until it does.

After bidding on a box of old books at an estate auction, I'm experiencing changes.

And I'm not talking about menopause.

My garden gnome Linda has come to life. No, really. Her name is Linda, and she never shuts up. A chonky cat with a few secrets of his own has adopted me. And a gorgeous professor of the occult tells me I'm a witch.

Right now, I'm not sure who's crazier—me, Linda or the hottie professor.

If this is my new reality, it's nature's cruel midlife trick. I'm learning fast that earth spells might be easy, but they aren't cheap. All magic exacts a toll, and if I don't master the elements, the elements will be the death of me.

Literally.

Chapter One

The garlicky scent of take-out created a nauseating stench I found hard to ignore. Now, I would forever associate Mongolian Beef with divorce, and it made me want to yark.

I passed the legal documents across the kitchen table to my lawyer Donald Overton III then glanced around my kitchen. "Sorry about the mess, Don." There were two plates, silverware, and cups in the sink, and it had been the third time I'd said I was sorry since his arrival.

"The place is cleaner than my house," he said.

Don, who was a six-foot-four man with rounded shoulders and a big, balding head to match, wasn't just my lawyer. He was also my brother-in-law. Which meant I knew he was stretching the truth to spare my feelings. My sister Rose was a meticulous housekeeper. "Is that it?" I asked.

He gave me a sympathetic look, emphasis on the *pathetic*, and nodded. "That's it, Iris. Done is done."

I rubbed my face. "Done is done," I repeated. "I'm officially Iris Everlee." I'd legally changed it a few weeks earlier. Still, it hadn't felt definitive that I was no longer a Callahan until I'd signed the divorce papers.

I'd wasted eighteen years married to a man who left me for someone else. Someone younger. Someone male. My ex, it turned out, was bisexual. I have always been open-minded. I genuinely believe, love is love and that people should live their truths. But when it's your husband, it's a lot harder to be congratulatory about someone discovering their "authentic self."

"Thanks for bringing those to me." I stood up from the table. "I have to get Michael up for practice."

Michael was my seventeen-year-old son. I worried he'd suffered the most during the divorce. But my son had always been a quiet child, not distant or anti-social, just even keel and low drama. It made it extremely difficult to gauge his real feelings most of the time.

"Is he still playing football?" Don asked.

"Yep. Today's the first day of spring training."

Don added, "You look like you need a friend. You should call Rose."

Unable to shake the feeling of trepidation, I said, "I'm fine. I'll be okay."

Don gave me a grim smile, then gathered up the paperwork and slipped it into a folder. "I'll get these filed at the courthouse today. You and Michael should come to dinner tomorrow night."

I stood up and walked him out of the kitchen and through the living room to the front door. "I'll call Rose later. I promise," I told him, which had been the only promise Don had been trying to extract. Of course, I hadn't promised *when* I would call.

"Please do. You know how Rose gets." My brother-in-law gave me a gentle shoulder squeeze, then left.

I had three sisters and one brother. Rose, the youngest of us all, had taken on the responsibility as the family worrywart since our mother died of pancreatic cancer five years earlier. The doctors had given her three or four months to live, but she'd died three weeks later in her sleep because the cancer had strangled her aorta and caused an aneurysm.

I closed the door and made my way down the dark hallway past the kitchen. Even with the door closed, the foul scents of boy stink threatened to knock me off my feet. Garlic leftovers had nothing on *Ewwww de Son*. I tapped on the door. No response. I pounded my fist against the wood. Still no response.

I opened the door a crack. "Hello?" I leaned on the door to open it wider as the sickly sweet and sour odors hit me full force, burning the back of my nostrils.

My eyesight adjusted to the dark. I saw a small mountain of dirty clothes wedged behind the door, barring further entry. I could see long toes peeking over the edge of a queen-sized mattress. Otherwise, I wouldn't have known a human being occupied the bed.

"Michael, damn it." Lately, "damn it" had been his middle name. "Let me in."

"What do you want?" came his muffled voice full of sleepy annoyance.

"I want you to open this stupid door right now."

"Go away."

"I'll go away. I'll go away to the garage and get a screwdriver and a hammer and take this freaking door off its hinges." Screw this. I pushed the door as hard as I could. Mount Dirt & Grime slid across the carpet and allowed me entry.

His foot drifted out of sight. He was moving—another good sign.

"What the hell died in your room? It smells like a serial killer's drop zone."

The boy sat up, his short hair looking too perfect to be slept in, just like his father. He scratched his patchy goatee. "Dramatic much?" His voice, low and pleasant in tone, held an edge of sarcasm.

I fought back a smile. My kid was beautiful, no doubt about it. He was one of the few things Evan and I had done right.

He blinked his soft brown eyes in my direction. "I'm not going to practice."

"Oh, you're going." I picked up a pair of sweatpants, a green pair at the top of the pile, and chucked them at him. "Get dressed."

He groaned and threw himself onto the bed, pulling the covers over his shoulders. "I'm tired."

"You wouldn't be so tired if you weren't up all night playing video games with your buddies."

He grunted. Translation: *Whatever*.

"Michael Evan Callahan, you will get yourself out of bed this minute. You promised your father."

He moaned his dissent. "Coach is going to be there," he replied.

"If you want a relationship with your dad, you're going to have to come to terms with the fact that Coach Adam is a part of his life now." I sounded so reasonable, even to my own ears. Inside, I was screaming. It had been a year since Evan and I had separated, and most of the time, I tried to not hate him for what he'd done to our family, but sometimes I struggled with taking the higher road.

"Yeah, well, you didn't catch them going at it." He was sitting up now, rubbing the sleep from his eyes. "And you expect me to come to terms with it."

Unfortunately, my son had discovered his father's infidelity before me. He'd gone to talk to Coach Adam after school hours and found him and Evan kissing in the coach's office. Michael had come home and locked himself in his bedroom that night. I could still see his hurt and rage. Being caught by our kid was what prompted Evan to finally come clean with me.

Sighing, I sat on the bed next to Michael and put my hand on his shoulder. "Kissing is not going at it," I said.

My oldest sister Dahlia was a family counselor. She'd recommended someone for the family to see, including Evan, in order for us to move forward with our lives.

"Close enough," he countered.

It took months for Michael to even look at his father, then a few months more for him to have a civil conversation with him. I was angry with Evan, but still, I was glad that Michael was finally seeing him again. They'd been taking it slowly. A few lunches and dinners here and there. One month ago, their relationship had taken another setback when Evan and Adam decided to go public and move in together.

I missed the days when I could scoop Michael into my arms and cuddle him. He was at that age now where he would have pulled away if I tried to comfort him. As it was, I could feel him shrink at my consoling touch. How could I expect him to understand and accept his father's new life when I could hardly think about him without my own rage clouding my mind? I felt like I'd wasted my best years on him. He'd promised to love me until *death do we part*. Yes, I lost my husband, but I'd also lost my best friend. Evan and I had more in common than anyone I'd ever met. We had the same tastes in books, music, and movies. We'd shared similar political and philosophical beliefs, and we'd rarely ran out of conversation.

On top of that, our sex life had been good. Don't get

me wrong, we'd had our share of arguments. It's hard to be with someone for eighteen years and not have any fights, but we'd always made up. In other words, his falling in love with someone else, regardless of gender, had been a complete blindside.

"Michael," I said, my voice gentle but strained. "I understand that you're uncomfortable around your dad and Adam but avoiding them is not going to make your life any better or easier. Do you want a relationship with your father?"

The teenager raised a wary brow. "Don't shrink me, Mom. That's what you pay Dr. Bradford for."

I narrowed my gaze. "Well, do you? Do you want a relationship with your father? And keep in mind, he's the only father you have." I wasn't above deploying mommy-guilt. "Your dad changed your diapers, coached your baseball and basketball teams. He attended every sporting event you ever played in high school. And he loves you," I said with as much gentleness as I could manage. "Now tell me, do you want a relationship with your father? Yes or no?"

"Sure," he said more than a little grudgingly. "But not with Coach."

"I'm not trying to make you have a relationship with Adam, but he and your father are a package right now." The words, even from my own lips, were a punch in the gut. Evan was a package with someone else now, and like Michael, I had to find a way to come to terms with it.

My teenaged son grunted. Unsympathetically, I clapped my hands to get his attention. "Get. Up."

Earth Spells Are Easy

"I hate you," he said through gritted teeth as he clambered from the bed.

I tried not to let the hurt show on my face. There were plenty of times I'd thought the same words to my mother when I was a teenager, but I never meant it, and I reminded myself as I let out a slow breath that Michael didn't mean it either. "You can hate me all you want, son, just as long as you mind me."

After dressing, and before he left the house, Michael gave me a rare hug and mumbled "love you" in my ear.

"I know," I said. "Love you more." And out the door he went. Once I was alone, my breath started coming faster, harder, and my pulse kicked up a notch—a feeling I knew all too well. This was the beginning of a panic attack. I tried to slow my exhales through pursed lips. *Blow out the candle*, I told myself, as I raced for the back door.

I quickly shoved it open and staggered into my floral paradise, aka my backyard garden. It was a brilliant mixture of colorful wildflowers and herbs. *Cleome and zinnias to attract butterflies and hummingbirds*, my mother had said when she'd help me plan the garden. There were yarrow plants for ladybugs. And fennel and dill, which are supposed to attract beneficial insects, but frankly, after all these years, I couldn't remember which bugs were good. I'd turned the fountain on in the spring, and the sound of trickling water started to soothe my anxiety.

I sat on a bench near a patch of garden phlox. The plants were all green now, but in July, delicate, pale-pink flowers would cluster in bunches. I put my elbows on my knees and lowered my head.

Linda stared at me with contempt. I flipped her off. She didn't react. Of course, she wouldn't. Linda was a stone garden gnome. I'd turned her around the night before, so she was staring at the dill and not at the bench. But—I was guessing—Michael had moved her to mess with me. The kid loved freaking me out. It was his new favorite game of let's see how many ways we can startle Mom.

Her beady eyes always creeped me out. More than once, I'd contemplated tossing her out, but she'd been a gift from my mother.

Every garden needs a gnome, she'd told me. *And this sweet girl will keep your garden lush.* Like a mini-Santa, the gnome had a snow-white beard. Mom had painted its hat and tunic pink.

"How do you know it's female?" I'd asked my mother.

"Oh." She'd given me a knowing look. "She's full of feminine energy." My mother had tapped her chest. "I can feel it in here."

I could've done without a gnome, but Mom loving the ugly statuette had softened my feelings toward the little creature.

"What now?" I asked Linda. "What do I do with my life now?"

I waited for a few seconds for a response I knew would never come. A rustle in the bushes drew my attention away from my stone nemesis. Two long ears twitched above a small rosemary bush, followed by the rest of the rabbit. It was much larger than an Eastern cottontail and smaller than a desert jackrabbit. I'd seen it several times since the beginning of spring, and I wondered what in my garden kept the little fella coming back.

I stood up and narrowed my gaze on my recurrent garden guest. "Hello, Bunny Foo-foo?"

The rabbit, reddish-brown in color, twitched its nose at me. The hair on my head and my arms raised as if the air had turned staticky around me. Only, there was hardly any breeze this morning. The rabbit scurried back behind some bushes, and by the time I walked over, I saw a burrowed-out spot under my privacy fence. The electric tingle I'd felt had disappeared with the small bushy-tailed beast.

I began to look up types of hares on my phone when it rang, saving me from going down that proverbial and literal rabbit hole. I smiled as the name of the caller flashed on my screen. It was my second to oldest sister, Marigold.

"Hey, sis," I answered. "What's up?"

"What are you doing tomorrow night?" she asked. No, how are you? No, sorry about your divorce. I loved that about my hippy-dippy sister. She knew how to avoid a sore subject.

I grinned. "I'm watching *Hospital Blues*. It's a new episode."

She sighed. "That's what DVRs are for. You can record it. Is there anything you can't get out of?"

I made a mental calculation of all the things I had to do this week, including anything involving work or Michael, and couldn't think of a darn thing. He was old enough now to drive himself to practices, and I'd finished editing "Don't Let Your Participle Dangle," a follow-up textbook to "Where Did I Misplace My Modifier?"

I used to be a professor of English out at Darling University, located just outside my hometown of Southill Village in the Ozark Mountains in Northern Arkansas near the Missouri border. I quit when Michael was born and had been working from home, living the glamorous life of a textbook editor ever since.

Unfortunately, I wouldn't have my next assignment until June tenth, so I didn't have a reason to say no to Marigold. "Is washing my hair a good excuse?"

Her tone was bright. "Not even in the slightest. Dress casual," she said. "I'll pick you up at four-thirty."

"So early? What are we doing?"

"There's an estate auction going on in New Weston. We are going to bid on something eccentric and fun."

"We're going to do what?" I grabbed my coffee from the counter and sat down at my dining room table."

"Going to an estate auction. Ruth Boothwell died three months ago without any heirs, and her estate is auctioning off loads of fancy stuff."

"Fancy stuff, huh?" I asked skeptically. "Look, Mar. I don't have time to go to an estate auction."

"Come on, Iris. What else have you got planned?"

"Washing my hair. Shaving my legs. Waxing my mustache."

Marigold laughed. "It's about time. Self-care is the first step in reclaiming your life. But you can do that tonight. Besides, this is more than just a leisure trip. A colleague of mine, Professor Keir Quinn, has written a book and needs a good editor before he starts submitting it to publishers."

Marigold taught Women's Studies at Darling U. She, like me, had gone the academia route. This wasn't the first time she'd asked me if I would look at a "friend's" manuscript. The last one she'd asked me to look at had been a romantic thriller set in South Florida. I'd given it a hard pass.

"I don't know how many times I have to tell you that I don't do fiction, but...I don't do fiction."

Of course, I read fiction for pleasure, but I didn't want to have to ponder if a comma should exist in a sentence or if it was a choice the writer made to leave it out. Same with sentence fragments and other style issues that might or might not be on purpose. I liked the grammatical and mechanical clarity in which textbooks were written.

"I know you don't do fiction," Marigold shot back. "So, it's a good thing Keir's writing is of the non-fiction variety."

"Mills & Laden Academic Press sends me plenty of work to keep me busy."

She sucked her teeth, producing a sound of sheer annoyance. "I know you only get one book a month, and I also happen to know that you are amazingly fast at your job. Besides, you could use extra money right now, right? And this guy is willing to pay double your normal fees."

I sat down and closed my eyes as I prayed for patience, then asked, "Why would he do that?"

"Because Keir needs it done fast. You know how it is at universities. Publish or perish. Besides, it's an easy gig." My sister sounded exasperated with me. "You should take it."

"It's only easy if he's a half-decent writer."

"He is," Marigold assured me. "Look, come with me to the auction. Talk to the man. And if you decide to turn down the job, no harm, no foul."

The divorce, even with the sister-in-law lawyer discount, had been costly. I wondered if Rose had reached out to Marigold, and the two of them had cooked up this scheme to help me financially. I did need the money. And aside from that, even if I decided not to take the gig, going to an estate auction might be fun. The idea of getting out and doing something that wasn't work, kid, or husband—I shook my head at my mental slip—ex-husband—related stirred excitement in me.

"Fine," I finally said. "What time should I pick you up tomorrow?"

"I can drive," she protested.

"Barely," I told her. "Do you want me to go or not?"

I heard her harrumph. "I'll come over to your house at four, but you can drive," she said before I could protest. "The auction starts at five-thirty, but I want to get there early enough to check out the sale items."

"I'll be ready with bells on."

"Excellent," she said. "And Iris..."

"Yeah?"

"You know if you want to talk...about today or whatever, I'm here for you."

I nodded even though she couldn't see me. "I do know. Love you, sis."

"Love you back."

Read Earth Spells Are Easy today!

ABOUT THE AUTHOR

I am a USA Today Bestselling author who writes paranormal mysteries and romances because I love all things whodunit, Otherworldly, and weird. Also, I wish my pittie, the adorable Kona Princess Warrior, could talk. Or at least be more like Scooby-Doo and help me unmask villains at the haunted house up the street.

When I'm not writing about mystery-solving werecougars or the adventures of a hapless psychic living among shapeshifters, I am preyed upon by stray kittens who end up living in my house because I can't say no to those sweet, furry faces. (Someone stop telling them where I live!)

I live in Mid-Missouri with my family and I spend my non-writing time doing really cool stuff...like watching TV and cleaning up dog poop

Follow Renee!
Bookbub
Renee's Rebel Readers FB Group
Newsletter

Made in United States
Cleveland, OH
29 July 2025